Dave
Bi-Plane

Fights the Red Winged Death Command

S.B. Norton

GRIMPRINT
PUBLISHING

From S. B. Norton check
out the very first instalment from
the world of Sombre!

SOMBRE

GRIMPRINT

PUBLISHING

First published 2021 by Grimprint Publishing

ISBN 978-0-646-84799-3

Dedicated.

To the Norton–Wallace's

To Michelle for planting the idea in my head for this one.

To my kids, Spencer and Lucy,
for being brainy buggers' who love to read.

Love you all.

CHAPTER 1
JASPER REEVES

Jasper Reeves was done for the afternoon.

He stood holding his board by the nose and sucked his bottom lip. Little kids and babies had invaded the skate park. Sunday learner bedlam. Kids knelt and pushed, rode scooters into the middle of the flat and stopped; unapologetic moms ran out and rescued fallers – it was all fairly hopeless.

Jasper watched on as a few fools that actually could skate; a couple of bike guys as well, stayed and tried their utmost to steer around the invasion. It wasn't for him. Too dangerous.

With a shrug, he turned the volume up on his earbud and walked off as D.R.I. blasted his ears with 'I Don't Need Society' – circa 1983. Just before the gate he dropped his board and rode. A warm sunny Arlington afternoon, a few clouds, the breeze picked up and he wiped his hair from his face. Crossing the road after a passing truck, he hopped the curb. He shot past the main street's cafes and bars without giving them so much as a glance. His music switched up to Suicidal Tendencies impassioned anthem, 'War Inside My Head'. He nodded his appreciation, one of the bands best in his humble opinion; getting lost in Mike Muir's urgent vocals and lyrical delivery.

Veering left onto Beaucombe Rd; he cruised the sloping sidewalk, the street all but completely bathed in the shadows of large, two storied housing, green manicured lawns, well clipped gardens and picket fences. At times he loved this street, with all its quiet comfort and polite suburbia. At other times, he thought himself an alien

1

intrusion, slicing through the perfect world exterior the families of the street seemed so desperate to advertise; feeling ten times the punk-skater-kid than he actually was.

Pulling up outside 4 Beaucombe Rd he grabbed his board and clicked the gate open. He gave the lawn a quick glance. The Reeves's garden was a little shameful compared to the rest of the street.

Mower duty for Jasper, any day now.

He stepped onto the verandah, killed the music and entered the house.

D

"Dad, you good?" Jasper called out, "is mom home?" All was quiet as he headed straight to the kitchen. He hated the quiet.

"No. Not yet. She rang though ... pizza tonight," came a voice from the lounge.

Jasper left the kitchen and entered the lounge with a handful of crackers. Looking to his father he nodded, "pizza's good I guess."

"Not great for the midsection though. I'm stacking it on at the moment. It's not like I can walk it off," said Tim Reeves raising his brow from behind a golf magazine.

His dad was in a wheelchair. At least he was at the moment. It was only a temporary thing Tim Reeves had assured them a week after the accident. The temporary thing was now ten months old. Therapy was slow.

"I'm heading to my room for a bit, you need anything?" Jasper said mid chew.

"I'm okay," he answered blandly as his eyes shifted back down to his mag.

With a nod, Jasper walked the short hall to his room. He shut the door, grabbed the remote and drowned the silence of the house with the fast and loud. His room was his haven. Bits of skateboards past and present littered the scuffed up floor-boards. Posters filled the walls: collector gig banners from all over the states and the rest of the planet, advertising thrash and punk shows at venues he had never been to (but would one day – a truth anyone could take to the bank) and skate pictures from bowls all over the world. An old Marantz turntable sat alongside his four-poster bed; a hand-me-down from his father for when he needed to hear that old school crackle of some of his favorites; a dock on his desk for when he didn't.

Pulling open his desk draw he grabbed a Snickers bar from his stash then collapsed on his bed. The playlist shifted to a heavier tune, 'Chalice of Blood' by Forbidden - circa 1988. Tapping his feet he chewed his chocolate and thought of his dad in the lounge. The music. It had all come from Tim Reeves - a mighty influence. Jasper knew he'd be in his chair nodding along as well. It was sad. Things had been hard since the accident, things had been hard all-round, for everyone.

"Jas', dinner!" his mother call out. He killed the music.

Ɗ

"The whole things been a bit of a useless and expensive pain in the ass - let's be honest. We need results, Tim. Cathy's not working out. I think it's high-time we look elsewhere. I want you up and about. She's had the best part of a year. She is a nice girl, but not-so-good as it turns out ..." Julie Reeves said downing the rest of her red wine. She ran her fingers through her blonde hair and pursed her lips. She reached for the bottle and refilled her glass.

"I can almost stand though – sometimes," Tim Reeves said, "it takes time, hon'. It was always going to."

"Can you stand, dad?" Jasper said curiously as he grabbed another slice, his last.

"Barely, Jas'." His mother scoffed rolling her eyes, "isn't a years' worth of physio there, let me tell you." She turned to Tim, "I just want you back, babe."

Jasper watched his father darken, "Yes, I know you do. You've had enough of Timmy the invalid, I know."

"Don't get like that, Tim. This is something you *can* recover from – it's not like we haven't friggin looked into it! I am just saying we look elsewhere so you can!"

Things went uncomfortably silent for a moment.

Jasper could see where this was going; his mother getting sozzled and more verbal, his father hating himself for something he had no control over. The arguing had been a once weekly occurrence over the last few months. The day it happened was generally random. Turns out Saturday night was the night for it this week. He didn't finish his last slice. Dropping it back on the plate he announced, "Anyway, think I'll let you two have it out. I'm off to my room – gonna hit the shower and turn in early."

"This is a discussion, Jas'. Adults have them you know," his mother said with a sniff.

"You guys just keep repeating the same shit over and over again. Don't really need to hear it. Want to get up early tomorrow and hit the park anyways," he said and kissed his mother's cheek. He gave his dad a short hug around the shoulders. "Take it easy. See ya."

"Night, dude," his dad patted his forearm.

4

CHAPTER 2
THE AIRMAN, DAVE BI-PLANE

Showered and in his bed-shorts, Jasper took a look at himself in the mirror. His arms were getting more definition to them; biceps, forearms – his chest expanding in the pectoral region as well. Joining the gym team had been a good idea – he figured it could only help the skating. He wasn't overly tall yet, 5'8 – but at 15, he had a few years left of growing to do. He liked his chest getting a bit of that barrel look, though. Not for any vanity reason, really.

More that it reminded him a little of the airman, Dave Bi-Plane.

He felt a kinship with the man.

The legend.

It didn't matter that Dave was a product of his dreams. Next to his father, he was the most admirable man Jasper knew.

Dave Bi-Plane was the shit.

And Jasper Reeves was the most level-headed kid Jasper Reeves knew – yet he allowed himself this part of his life willingly. Recently it was his life's mantra – to escape whenever he could. Three things let him do this: skating, music and *Sombre*.

Sombre and Dave Bi-Plane happened for the first time, on the night after the worst afternoon in his life, the day of Tim Reeves accident. It was one of those factory accidents you hear about, see reenactments of on lawyer ads during prime time – you just don't think it could ever happen to you or someone you're close to. Sometimes bad luck comes knocking – it came knocking for his father. A brainless act from a drug-addled forklift driver, his head chock-full of chemicals, left Tim Reeves pinned between two, two-ton pallets. So wasted was the driver he hadn't sensed the soft body obstructing the way - just kept pushing the double stacked pallet in place until it 'felt about right' - then apparently drove off, extremely effective noise cancelling ear protection cancelling out Tim Reeves's screams.

Prison time for Emmanuel, the driver.

Eight broken ribs, a fractured pelvis, broken ankles and so far, irreparable nerve damage to the lower half of his father's body. There was a lawsuit and pending court case next week for his father with Draker Foods - his place of employ for the past twenty years. Tim Reeves sat on the company's board. It was going to be messy. Costly mess all round. To the tune of millions.

On the night of the accident, after an eight-hour stint at the hospital; a stressed-out and exhausted Jasper dreamt of the dangerous nightmare world of Sombre and the airman, Dave Bi-Plane, for the very first time. Coincidental? He thought not. Sombre was meant for him - of that he was certain.

With a rhino-like yawn, he flopped onto the bed, switched his bedside light off and shut his eyes. Within minutes, he slept.

Jasper's Rite of Passage nightmare into Sombre took hold.

D

Arlington is empty. It's deep night. Street lights are non-operational. The houses sleep. Aiding moonlight completely obscured by inky black sky. An unimaginable time to be out skating. It's cold and he's shivering. It's been raining; the roads are wet as he travels straight up the middle. Not in the left, not in the right; the middle. His wheels sound hollow as they roll; he pushes steadily.

He waits. He knows they are coming. Nothing yet.

They will hurt him. Rightly or wrongly, he feels at peace with it. He knows it has to happen.

This is his Rite of Passage.

Following the road he turns left and enters the main street he has used at least a thousand times in reality's daytime. Surveying the deserted strip; the dark shop fronts promise no haven for Jasper Reeves - the strange kid out and about - skating at witching hour, a willing lone target.

From behind, a sound of clapping footfalls from boots with metal soles. Harried whispers of communication fill the area; brilliant in clarity yet barely intelligible. He can only make out the sporadic use of his name.

He pushes harder, rolls faster, heart beating in double time. He feels them at his shoulder. Bootsteps drumming in almost military precision. He won't outrun them. No chance.

The first strike from a front runner - a chrome plated baseball bat smashes his right knee and he falters; he howls with pain, heavy and dense.

Somehow, he stays upright.

Until he takes a second blow.

To the head.

It all disappears, the Rite of Passage complete.

D

Rotary motor purring in a most agreeable fashion, the Sopwith Camel flew over the canyon-esque expanse of The Panopticom Gateway, soaring into red sunlight. Dave Bi-Plane gave The Kestrel more stick and it obeyed. He smiled, rubbed his stubbly chin and adjusted his goggles.

The Gatherer's mission was complete. Not wildly successful, but sometimes they weren't – Dave had given up worrying about such things. In Sombre, gathering any Nightmarer still in one piece was an achievement in itself. The girl was whole, quite mutilated in the facial area, but something The Menders could work with, surely.

Dave had literally swiped her from the jaws of a Minotaur; with his trusty lasso that he was so very quick with. It had all been rather skillful: a pinpoint landing in copter-mode, a splash of his boots down in shallow water, the shooting of a wild Centaur straight between the eyes, and the aforementioned lassoing of the Nightmaring girl from the clutches of a Minotaur. The element of surprise sometimes worked in Sombre, particularly in a mythologically insular area like The Panopticom' (a nod to the archaic if there ever was one), a spinning propeller and wings not exactly what beasts of that nature were used to. Warring and bloodthirsty they were; machinery savvy they definitely were not.

The beast's teeth had torn the young redhead's face clean off. She awaited her inevitable mending, locked up safe, bleeding away in the slide-coffin at the back of The Kestrel's well-appointed fuselage.

'The Kestrel' was the name he had chosen for the biplane. Mainly because he thought it needed it. With a surname of 'Bi-Plane' he thought his aircraft could use its own identity – after all, The Kestrel was quite the marvel in its own rite. It was a moniker he shared with no one, mind you. Dave, for the most part was a simple fellow - a gentleman among a nightmare world of scavengers - but he did have his secrets, quite a number of them.

8

The scenery soon changed to a familiar darkness as he swung the biplane into a dive. The Funneling; the rushing, screaming wind chasm to The Office of The Menders presented in a maelstrom of turbulence. He controlled his craft with a well-practiced hand.

The wind lulled and he landed The Kestrel in a pitch-black dwelling one wouldn't exactly call a room nor an outer area. It was always quiet though, ominously cold and made him shiver, despite his thick leathers. The Funneling appeared differently for the kind of Gatherer you were. Dave was a rare one; the only one to actually fly a plane. There was plenty of aircraft in Sombre, too many to mention truth be known - but Gatherers used airships and air balloons – Dave was a solitary plane flyer among the throng of Sombre's dedicated servants.

"Come on girl, let's get you sorted," he said with a sigh that was neither indifferent nor overly caring - this was work. He lifted the lid on The Kestrel's fuselage and pulled on the handle of the slide-coffin. The dead Nightmarer presented, face gored to horrible extremity. Grimacing, he lifted the young girls corpse out by the shoulders; a weighty drag that ended with her bare feet hitting the concrete with a bony thud.

"No dignified way to do this my friend," Dave muttered as he braced the girl tight under the torso with his right arm.

With the unmistakable (and quite overbearing) variety of bloody-cadaverous and chemical stenches drifting up his nasal passages, the burly Gatherer walked her toward the double wooden doors of The Office of The Menders.

CHAPTER 3
THE CHOPPED-UP CLOCK SHOP

Controlled bedlam probably was not the best way to describe it, yet really was the only term that came to mind when one watched the service of The Office of The Menders. Dave stood at the doorway of the vast, rectangular room. A large, single-handed clockface adorned the far wall as if monitoring the proceedings like a great metal eye. A pile of Beating Clocks; the Sombre citizens replacement chest organ, sat plated in golds and silvers, stacked on the floorboards in the rooms centre.

On long gleaming surgical benches, Menders worked with speed and deft skill as blood flowed and was washed away. All manner of surgical procedure; simple face stitching to microbiologic and mind-blowing rebuilds of mutilated and scattered limbs; chest procedures from the intricate to the relatively simple resetting of a stroke on a Beating Clock.

Everything that existed in Sombre (at least everything with a Beating Clock) be it human, monster or animal - was serviced by the overworked Menders.

Not realizing he was in a bit of a daze; Dave startled a little as the Chief Mender, Hamish, appeared before him with his usual generous grin - particularly generous given his burden as the head of The Office of the Menders.

"Dave Bi-Plane. Good to see you. Who do we have here?" Hamish looked down at the slumped girl in Dave's arms. "She seems in good shape."

10

"You haven't seen her face yet," Dave said raising his eyebrows, he gave Hamish a doubtful look. "I think I might drop her on that spare spot on the bench. The poor thing is getting a little heavy."

"So how has business been at your Chopped-Up-Clock-Shop, Hamish?" Hoisting her up, he positioned her on her back and swept her red locks from what was left of her face. "There, told you not to get too excited by the state of this one."

Hamish lent over the girl and studied her devastated skull. "Busy ... yes, oh well, I will still give you a solid 7 out of 10 for your efforts here. Where were you?"

"The Panopticom Gateway, the borough with the mythological beasties. This is the work of the dreaded Minotaur," Dave said.

"What did you kill there?" Hamish said as he pushed with his first two fingers at what would have been the girl's jawbone had it not been ripped away.

"Just a Centaur. An easy fix for you. One shot to the head."

"Thanking you sir." Hamish said giving Dave an approving nod. "We appreciated the easy fix, as you know." He then looked the airman in his green eyes as if searching for something. "So how has it all been in general for you Dave Bi-Plane? Out of all the Gatherers in Sombre, you have always been the hardest for me to read. Call me nosey if you like but I do try to keep some form of communication up with you all." He gestured to the room around them, "This isn't just a Nightmarer drop off zone for you all. I mean it *is* that, but it is also the closest thing you will ever have to a place of care." He pointed to his chest, "Your stroke rate, Dave?"

"You're a good man, Hamish," Dave said giving the Mender a wink. He unzipped his jacket displaying his Beating Clock face. "I've been at four for a while now, and I plan to stay on four for as long as I can. Had a bad run there and lost a couple as you know."

"So, no troubles then?" he pried.

Dave chuckled incredulously, "Why would you want me to have any, man! Don't you have enough on your plate? There really is no need to delve into my lot. I'm okay. I'd rather not give you any reason for concern."

"True. I should be thankful. You are by far the most solid and reliable we have here in Sombre. It is appreciated, don't get me wrong. I'm always curious about you that's all."

Dave gave Hamish a reassuring nod, "Don't waste your valuable mind thinking about me, Hamish. I'm fairly simple. I fly a plane. I like a lager. I keep my nose clean. I take calculated risks only."

Hamish huffed, "I'm sure there is a lot more than that to you, Dave, but fair enough. I'll stop. Until next we meet." He turned and focused his attention on the new Nightmarer. Sliding her body along the steel bench he waved other Menders over for assistance.

Dave watched on as the girl was swallowed into the system. Nightmarer's, always the first priority in The Office of The Menders. Another troubled sleeper birthed into Sombre. The girl would be a new citizen, with her own Beating Clock in her chest, about to start her journey, her time in Sombre for as long as her citizens twelve strokes might last. Who or what she would become was anyone's guess.

Dave turned and sauntered to the doors – he wasn't about to stick around to find out. It really was of no concern to him. That wasn't part of the job. He gathered them, that was all.

D

The skies of Sombre were the familiar light and shadow show of coffee coloured clouds, brilliant sun and patches of illuminated grey. Dave flew The Kestrel at a nice and easy 80 mph.

A pale pink envelope appeared up ahead, black basket beneath carried its pilot. A shot of red gas flame. He drew level with the 'Bexley' balloon, and he gave the woman a wave. Hanging on the ropes, she signaled back to Dave, dropping two fingers toward ground as she began her descent. Recalcitrance Bexley, a fellow Gatherer; a drinker, a smoker, an all-round agreeable person. She was as sharp as they came. She would be on her way to The Ruptured Spleen for refreshment no doubt. His mouth felt dry. He was definitely tempted, but he thought better of it. The Kestrel needed a clean, and he was sure he heard a slight misfire somewhere in the motor. The rotary seven cylinder – horribly unreliable regardless at how meticulous one was with its maintenance. Back to base. He left the balloonist in his wake and flew on.

His thinking went to the meeting he just had with Hamish and he grinned. The man was certainly prying! More than he had done for a while as well.

The mystery. Hamish wanted in on it. Dave huffed. It wasn't just his well-being! It was the mystery. The mysterious history of Dave Bi-Plane, the history of his own self. As the fifth Dave Bi-Plane, *he* even found it intriguing. He was more than just a name. He knew of the jocular way his surname had come about (being named after his transport). It achieved the odd smirk amongst Gatherers, but that was all. He was well considered among the throng as a rule.

"What on earth?" roused from his thoughts, he startled as his cockpit radio hissed into life. He stared at the device. The radio was rarely used, basically an ornament. Gatherer's kept to themselves in the air as a rule.

The transmission was gargle to begin with. Bleeps and burps and broken low rumblings. Whoever it was that were trying to contact him seemed to be coming from far away.

"This is interesting," Dave muttered. Beyond the sound of The Kestrel's motor, (which he could definitely now hear its need of tinkering), the transmission was getting a little clearer.

"What and who?" he lent in closer toward the radio. Did he just hear the word *'Bi-Plane'*? Were they talking about his aircraft, or did they mean him?

He listened for more.

There was more.

'Bi-Plane ...' crackle *'Where ...?'* crackle *'We've come ...'*

Whoever they were they were getting closer. And they definitely meant him. He picked up the sound of distant motors. Planes. Plural. There were plenty of them.

'Bi-Plane! Where is it?'

The transmission this time was crystal. The voices not quite human yet not quite beastly either – they all held the same deadly pitch, though.

A quick glance over his shoulder confirmed how many. About a mile away - the silhouettes of 6 Spitfire's.

Ahead, the gargantuan form of Sebastien Steppanaire's air palace loomed. Haven.

He swung the biplane left and approached the floating city-esque structure. Preparing for a conventional landing on the wildly ostentatious, black shining glass, he took a last harried look at his

14

pursuers, they had closed in quick. He turned back around and rode the control stick for a sideslip landing.

'*Where, Bi-Plane! We know you have it!*'

Pulling The Kestrel to a bumping, sharp stop he killed the engine and looked skyward.

The line of Spitfires flew by.

He saw the colour of the wings and for a moment, forgot to draw a breath.

Red.

He knew of them. They were legend. Infamous. He just never had encountered them before now. The Red Winged Death Command of Strom Pel.

"Of all the unrealities to befall someone."

Dave Bi-Plane didn't scare easily.

He was scared.

D

Jasper Reeves woke sitting upright on the mattress, looking straight ahead. He fell back on the pillow and smiled.

CHAPTER 4
WHEN NOTHING COMPARES

Jasper knew it probably was not the healthiest way to live – longing to go back to sleep every day. It was the case though. He couldn't do much about it. Dreaming of Sombre? Getting to be Dave Bi-Plane every night? Well, it was just about as awe inspiring as things could get.

Monday morning skate to school: track - Gorilla Biscuits – 'Good Intentions - 1989', blared away in his ears. He was half an hour earlier than he need to be - so he could grind the curbs and practice his street on the way. He thought of what had just happened to Dave. Those planes were awesome, and scary. They wanted something and he couldn't wait to find out what it was. The mystery was getting fairly juicy.

There was no dreaming like it. He had looked into it as well – after the first week of dreaming of Dave Bi-Plane, he took it upon himself to research plenty online and in the library. Trauma nightmares and Lucid dreaming were a real thing. Dreaming like he was in Sombre wasn't. He was living a night-time-only life right alongside his own. Just a hundred miles better life than his real one; with a dad stuck in a wheelchair and a passive aggressive, sort-of-bitter mother.

No, it wasn't healthy, he knew it. It was what it was. And what choice did he have anyway? It wasn't about to go away anytime soon. Afterall, Dave Bi-Plane was only on stroke four out of the twelve he had on his Beating Clock. He smiled at this as he Ollied a bench seat, rolled and dropped to the curb.

He had arrived, reality awaited.

Across the street, the shady gateway of Massa High School beckoned. With a sigh, he flipped his board, caught it by the nose and crossed the road. Sweeping his fringe from his brow, he turned the volume up on his phone as legendary skate punkers, the Spermbirds, blasted his ears with 'Shit Job'. He loved the fact that the band were German with an American born singer. The guy chose to go live over there with them; then spit nasty, abusive punk rock back at the States. Ultimate punk – real punk.

"Reeves", Josh Lancaster, the star quarterback for the Massa Devils crossed his path with his usual crew in tail. All tall and built like concrete pylons – sport machinery.

Jasper fist bumped them all.

He continued on and nodded at a group of girls that had turned his way as he walked the drive. Stacy, Emily, Bree, Heather – he knew they all would date him if he actually asked them. There were others in his year level as well; and he would be lying if he said he wasn't tempted, but he didn't need all the bullshit that would come with it.

Jasper had dated just once, in his freshman year, Simone, a four-month nightmare of emotional confusion, jealousy and strained conversation. He was older now and so were the girls, but it really wasn't a priority for him at the moment. Between skating, school-work, sport and all the stress at home with his folks, he had plenty on his plate - so thanks, but no thanks.

And nothing compared to Dave Bi-Plane and Sombre. An all-time, all-encompassing distraction. There was no room for friends, just acquaintances. Everyone got a 'hi', everyone got a 'see ya' – that was all.

Disappearing through the turn-styles he headed to class.

D

The topic had been the football team, the Massa Devils. The one something of interest to come out of his day at school. "There's been some scouts at the school lately," Jasper said. "They were there today – bunch of bigwigs."

Tim Reeves nodded. "I used to play Right Defensive, back in the day."

Jasper watched Tim Reeves as he placed his fork down on his plate and chewed his steak. He thought his father looked like a happy dwarf in the wheelchair this evening. He hated it. It probably wasn't the case, but he looked like he was wasting away.

Jasper gestured to Julie Reeves. "Mother, what say you? Was dad any good?" He raised his eyebrows and smiled knowingly. She couldn't have given a shit. She was far too concerned with the upcoming settlement and subsequent pay out the family would receive from her beau's injury. The sitting at the law offices of Baker and Finch was scheduled for the end of the week.

"Football. Think we have some college photos somewhere," she said and fell back into deep thought. Her eyes glazed over as she sipped her wine.

Jasper left the unanswered question alone as conversation had lulled. The Reeves family were just riding things out. The hearing was a quantifiable necessity, a life buoy floating in the mucky waters of the toughest eleven months the Reeves's had ever had. They all needed to take a unified sigh of relief. His mother needed to see a cheque with lots of zero's. The future after the settlement would bob along a little better on the yet undisclosed money cushion. That was the hope.

"Dad, do you have another therapy session tomorrow?" Jasper queried as he got up from the table.

"Indeed I do, and thank you for asking, Jas," he rubbed his beard then stretched. "Although, I am starting to agree with your mother ... progress is a bit too slow there. Cathy's doing her best – I think working with nerves might be a bit beyond her. I'm looking into some other avenues, we'll see." He gave them both what was meant to be a look of reassurance.

Jasper glanced over at his mother; she was dead still, her right hand holding the stem of her empty wine glass – she looked catatonic. "Anyway, I got homework," he said as he moved round the table and kissed them both on the cheek. Julie grabbed his wrist and gave it a squeeze. She was lucid; that was reassuring. He left the kitchen and headed to his room.

D

He had been surprisingly productive after dinner, tapping out a sub-par, first draft of an English essay. His rough take and opinion on the fall of printed text as opposed to digital media (the pros and cons of) was due before the end of the week.

With a satisfied stretch he closed his laptop and swiveled on his chair for a moment. His thoughts turned to the world of Sombre and Dave Bi-Plane. He recalled red wings. Spitfire airplanes. Dave had trouble. Flicking the lamplight off, he crossed the room and fell onto his mattress, disappearing under the covers.

Shutting his eyes tight he willed sleep to smother the world away.

CHAPTER 5
ABOARD SÉBASTIEN STEPPANAIRE'S AIR PALACE

As still as a corpse, Jasper's nightly adventure began once again.

His Rite of Passage nightmare into Sombre continuing right from where it had left off.

To early morning, on the streets of Arlington.

D

Jasper would never have been out at this hour normally; no one skated past midnight. Night made it near impossible to see what was under your wheels. Also who might come at you from the darkness. Mean you harm. This was only a dream. Dreams generally made no sense; he was definitely being made to pay for his misadventure in this one.

He had been allowed to get to his feet. Head pounding hard from the hit with the metal bat it hurt to open his eyes, so he squinted.

There were ten. Men and women. All dressed in black suits and heavy leather boots. All wore stark white makeup accentuated with an application of black makeup around the eyes - at the nose and around the mouth. Horrific, yet comical and deadly serious. Each were armed with a variety of weapons: machetes, the metal bats, fire torches and chain lengths.

He had his skateboard.

The games were about to begin.

"Well, this isn't fair is it?" He heard himself say. "What do you want?"

"You," said a woman in a voice twice as cold as the early morning air. "You, Jasper Reeves." Through her black lips, her teeth were shining metallic. "You're about to be beaten to death."

D

Was Dave Bi-Plane about to be hunted? It seemed that way.

The nightmare world of Sombre was certainly a dangerous one. Holding onto one's stroke's on a Beating Clock always quite the task as there was combat for a Gatherer on every mission - every sort of monster, deranged human-form, demon and unexplained entity. There was always a threat.

Yet, Dave could not recall ever being 'hunted' if that was what was happening.

He stood at the doorway of his garage cleaning a cylinder with a petroleum-soaked rag. He peered out at the goings on of Sebastien Steppanaire's air palace.

The air palace was definitely a wonder, a monumental intrusion on the surrounding skies. As lavishly palatial as any palace and more. The shiny black glass he stood on was a wonder in itself. And the man had his workers that was for certain. Strong men and women in neat collared white shirts and stiff black trousers. The diligent staff scaled and cleaned the walls of the palace's seven towers; buffed hundreds of windows to a sparkle. At ground level they tended to the many gardens and polished the floor with silk mops.

Dave Bi-Plane's own allotted space at the inner ward of the massive dwelling was also well appointed. He called it his garage, yet it really was so much more than that. His biplane sat parked in floorspace double its width; there was shelving and shadow boards for his many tools, ample room for his petroleum and oil. In the far corner was a small living quarter with swivel chairs, a kitchenette to make himself a strong black cup of tea on the occasion he required one and a bathroom with a bathtub and a pull curtain. The garage was even cleaned for him whilst he was out on missions.

As far as Dave knew Sebastien Steppanaire wasn't any sort of aristocrat that deserved such a dwelling. Why the man had any of this in the first place and who had indeed dreamt up such a thing to have it exist in Sombre was anyone's guess. All just one of the nightmare worlds many curiosities.

Dave appreciated it all mind you – and again, he never spoke of his home base to any other Gatherer. Not even to the likable but prying, Hamish.

There was a strumming of strings, barely musical, light and repetitive, played by unskilled fingers. Dave shook his head slowly and grinned as his attention went to his right. Like an overweight minstrel, Sebastien Steppanaire strolled the glass wearing a long, tan coloured fur gown and open toed shoes. The sound was from a ukulele; tiny in the large man's hands. He rested the main body of the instrument up on his Beating Clock. Although the clock hand was obscured, Dave knew it stroked at one. It had been at one for as long as he could remember. A man like Sebastien rarely ran into trouble in Sombre.

"David, how are you this evening? I thought the conditions wonderful for a walk and a practice. I'm awful at it, I know, yet like everything I do, my old foolish heart's in the right place, ha-ha!"

Dave watched the man's chin wobble as he laughed and tried his best not grimace. It was incredibly loose chin skin.

"I'm fine thank you, Sebastien. We don't hear a lot of music in Sombre, my hat goes off to you for giving it a go."

"It relaxes me," Sebastien said stopping mid strum.

Dave wondered if he said the right thing. The man appeared a little hurt. Should he have been more complimentary? He moved on.

"Tell me, Sebastien, did you happen to see me arrive this afternoon?"

"No. Why my good fellow? I would have been in the parlor arguing with my staff as usual ... was there something special? Did you blow a piston again?"

Sebastien ran a hand through his dark hair and flicked it out as if it were stuck and it irritated him. Dave tried not to smirk. "No, well actually, I *am* having to adjust a few things in the motor," he peered back at The Kestrel. He thought it could do with a clean. "No, the only reason I ask was that my arrival was definitely under duress. I was being chased down."

Sebastien gave him a confused look, "Who would be chasing you down, Dave? What in Sombre have you done? You aren't bringing trouble here? I would much rather you didn't."

Dave was a little taken aback at the reaction but didn't show it. He had been a fairly quiet resident at the palace over his stay. He stared the man in his eyes. "Not intentionally, no. You have been around for quite a time, Sebastien. Have you ever come across a group of flyers known as The Red Winged Death Command?"

Sebastien gave the ukulele a single strum. He muffled the strings and looked skyward, "Well, no I haven't. But please tell me you haven't been mission flying in Strom-Pel at all. No good can come of it. A troupe with a name like that would have to have been derived there, surely."

Sebastien's expression was stern. Like a fathers.

Dave was taken aback for the second time. "If I was called to go there, I would have to go, but no, I haven't ventured there at all."

He wasn't a child and didn't need telling off or any guidance at all from Sebastien Steppanaire. Indeed, the relationship between the two was merely payment; a transaction for services rendered. Sebastien swore he owed his very existence to Dave Bi-Plane, an over statement made from an, at times, overly emotional mound of a man.

It had happened eons ago now. The attack on Sebastien Steppanaire had been a cowardly act and Dave Bi-Plane had stepped in, a little too late as it turned out. It was the reason for Sebastien's one and only lost stroke on his Beating Clock.

The fourth Dave Bi-Plane, his predecessor, had been passing on a Gatherer drop. He flew by the Steppanaire Air palace often (it was hard not to run into given its size). On this occasion he spotted rising black smoke. There was obvious trouble. A rare thing. He had never known anything but stately calm from the palace up until then.

It was not in Dave Bi-Plane's nature not to help someone in need.

Dave had turned The Kestrel around immediately and dived down.

The Steppanaire palace was rare and valuable aero-estate – Dave had intruded on a savage and hostile bid to take it over. Black planes lined the glass flooring, Marauder flyer's from Strom-Pel, the very region Sebastien had just spoken of. Guns blazing, bombs exploding in all-out bombast. Unarmed ground staff were falling fast.

Swooping The Kestrel in low just above ground level he opened fire with his exaggerated Vickers gun and sprayed the scene, taking down the evil with deadly accuracy. Landing on a dime on the black glass, he leapt from the helm. Running into the foyer, charging up the marble staircase he discovered the owner, Sebastien, had been left on the stairs like bleeding trash, shot and bitten - quite dead, with a decorative sword in his grasp. He had tried to defend his house, his honour, his staff.

Aviators from Strom-Pel came in all forms; this breed was known as Infural-Alsatian, and no doubt working for a higher power in Strom-Pel. A nasty amalgam of high thinking human and savage animal; able to pilot craft, think with logic and use weaponry. The breed could then run all fours, hunt and rip open throats. Not the wildest fan of being on foot in such a volatile situation, Dave had shot ambidextrously with two exaggerated pistols. The details of the ensuing battle alluded him now as it was so long ago, but Sebastien was correct - anything from the air of Strom-Pel couldn't be a good thing.

"Anyway, Sebastien, I was only curious - nothing will come of it I am sure. And if by chance it does it will be kept away from the here, you needn't worry."

"Good. Thank you, Dave." With a nod, Sebastien continued on with his stroll of the grounds with a strum.

"I just wonder what they want with me?" Dave said to himself as he turned and headed back into the garage. He held the offending cylinder up at eye level. "You look in okay shape, let's get you back in there, eh."

It was time to get in the air.

He was dry. He needed a lager.

Chapter 6
Thirst, the Ruptured Spleen

'Where is it Bi-Plane!'

He eyed the crackling radio. The Red Winged Death Command. The transmission coming from miles away. Thankfully he was almost where he needed to be.

Was this going to be the way it was every time he took to the air? He very much doubted he could out-fly a gang of Strom-Pel Spitfires in any way, whatsoever.

Where was it? What were they after? Subconsciously, he avoided the question.

Instead he listened to the mechanized thrum of The Kestrel. The motor did sound better after a bit of tinkering from its owner. Dave knew his biplane was considered a dinky little sky-farter by many a Gatherer (although no one ever said this to his face). Small minded opinions held no interest for him, his transport was his everything. Far quicker than a balloon or airship, the cabin was quick to get out of, and it did have its extra advancements. One of which he knew defied any kind of logic: Copter Mode – The Kestrel could go straight up and go straight down. Constraints of all rational gravity and aerodynamics be damned, all were taken with a pinch of salt in Sombre. Vehicles existed as everything else did in the Nightmare world, to suit Sombre's need. He would use Copter Mode now as he flew out of Common Air-Space and into the permanent twilight that shrouded The Unexplained Mountain. Resting on the mountain's peak, unremarkable, dim lights in its bay windows, the cigar box-shaped structure that was The Ruptured Spleen beckoned. The Gatherer's oasis. Patrons were out drinking on the north-facing verandah.

He swallowed dryly; he was damned thirsty.

Parking was scarce at the mountain's base. Peering down at balloon canvas's, airship dirigibles and a variety of land vehicles, he sought a break of empty land. He spotted the machanihorse, Wilder, Halliday Knight's impressive mechanical mare, meandering around between a Speed Truck and a group of Speed Cycles, rows and rows away from the entry. There appeared a few feet there he could park The Kestrel. Wilder would make way. Slowing the motor, he pushed on the downward throttle with an open hand and dropped his craft down. The machanihorse trotted sideways as he knew she would.

D

Elevator doors opened to the wonderfully familiar sounds of The Ruptured Spleen. Smells of hops and spirit, frying oil, sweat and cologne invaded Dave's nostrils as he hung his helmet and goggles. Pushing on the twin entry doors, he entered the bar.

He headed straight to the barkeep. "Orty, how are you this evening? My usual would be a charm my good man." Dave smiled not expecting any words in return. Orty rarely spoke, serving drinks like a machine his only real port of call. Giving the airman a nod of his bald head, Dave had his frothy lager sliding his way in seconds. "Thank you, you are a rock-solid marvel of a man."

Taking a long swig of the brew, he canvassed the bar really only seeking one individual. Halliday Knight. She would be one to talk to about this new dilemma. Whether she had anything helpful to suggest, or even how much the woman would actually take in, was always dependent on how many of her beloved scotch and dry's she had downed. She was his favorite Sombre native – and always had been apparently. There really was no one else he would rather speak to.

What appeared to be a rather serious game of poker was underway in the far corner. At first, he only saw the black spiky hair of one Recalcitrance Bexley. The balloon Gatherer was standing shoulder to shoulder with others, watching on intently. She blew a quick puff of cigarette smoke into the air. He drifted over. Generally, Halliday was never far from Recalcitrance. The two women complimented each other well.

Halliday Knight was generally troubled, in trouble or causing trouble.

Recalcitrance was a lover of all trouble. She did it all with a certain clever style and substance as well, which Dave admired. Dave drew level with the Bexley woman. He was half a head shorter – not an overly tall fellow was Dave Bi-Plane.

"Recalcitrance, how are you this evening? Have you seen Halliday?" He looked in at the game and wasn't surprised to see two opposing airship captains in fierce combat. He found the type to be the most deluded in all of Sombre – it seemed there was always an ultimate sky supremacy thing going on within each airship enterprise. Captain Mortdecai Drake, the other, Captain Stan Dawdle. The game wasn't poker as he first thought – in fact, he wasn't entirely sure what it was. Each had a glass tumbler and a tall bottle of Witches Still vodka; there was hard drunken staring and psyching of the other out, the turn of a card from a deck, showing it - one winning - one losing -

one taking not just a shot, but a full throat of vodka. Dave noticed Mortdecai's Beating Clock was stroking high at 10.

"She's in the toilet," Recalcitrance answered not looking away from the spectacle. "Sorry Dave, the stupidity of this game I am finding mesmerizing."

"No. Fair enough. It is extremely stupid," he agreed just as Captain Stan apparently lost the card flip and poured another glass with a shaky hand. He downed the drink, grinned, expelling air through his lips at the same time. Members of his crew applauded.

Dave turned as he felt a tap on the shoulder.

"Well, hello Dave Bi-Plane."

A grinning Halliday Knight stood behind him, drink in hand. He gave her what he thought his most charmed expression; bemusement with a smattering of surprise. "Halliday, how are we this evening?"

It did him no good to get carried away at all with her beauty, it would be far too easy, and far too hard to recover from. Her long blonde locks, agreeable mouth and bluest eyes were set perfectly in her heart shaped face; Halliday was a statuesque and powerful build yet not intimidating – he'd never seen her in anything but her knee length white dress and tough black boots. Her Beating Clock stroked at four, like his own.

"Are you watching this stupid game as well, Dave? It is some dopey stuff they are doing. Recalcitrance seems quite taken with it," Halliday said raising an eyebrow.

"Actually, no. I would like to chat. Shall we move to the verandah and take in some air, Halliday?" Dave gestured for them both to leave Recalcitrance to her fascination.

"She'll grow bored of it shortly, I am sure," Halliday said as they both stepped into the twilight outside. "Have you had any good gather's lately, my Dave?"

How he did appreciate it when she called him 'my Dave' - he rubbed his mouth in a bid to wipe away his grin. "No. Nothing of note. Lots of dead ones. You?"

Turning round she leant her back on the verandah railing and took a sip from her straw before answering. "The Lacerateral Industrial area, was where I was last. After searching factory after factory, dodging all those random, mechanized, tumbling-blade-balls, as you have to, the stupid fellow awarded my efforts by jumping head first into one of those unsavoury knife point roller machines. The bugger actually somersaulted in, like it was an Olympic-moment!"

Dave let out a laugh. He did appreciate Halliday's delivery of a story. "How did you clean up that?"

"Called the Menders. He was scattered and smattered all through the rollers - so I left them to it." She peered down at her empty tumbler and sighed; "It was quite the failure ..." She waved the glass his way, "... so I need another of these."

Dave downed the rest of his. "Let's walk and talk our way to the bar, shall we? You never know when we'll be called to duty."

"We shall, my Dave," she agreed and made toward the glass doors. "So, what is new in the Sombre skies?"

He stayed in close at her side, "Halliday, I think I am being hunted."

She gave him a quizzical look. "Hunted? How so?"

"Exactly that."

"That is most unusual, my Dave. Who did you irritate?" Halliday placed her empty onto the bar. "Orty, drink for me please. Give it a good mix, man. One for Dave as well." She turned, leant on the bar and studied him. "Actually, scratch that thought. I irritate plenty a citizen and have never been targeted by a single one. Ha! Come to think of it, they wouldn't dare." She raised her eyebrows. "Who are these hunters, man." She took both drinks from Orty eyeing the strength of her own closely as she passed Dave his lager. They moved through the rowdy bar. The strange card game between the airship captains appeared to be drawing to a close. From the sound of all of the 'whoa's!' and 'ahhh's!', one or the other were about to collapse.

He sipped from his second lager, "Flyers, Halliday - from Strom-Pel. The Red Winged Death Command."

The two stepped out onto the verandah once again. Dave took a long breath.

"Well they definitely *sound* like trouble, my Dave. Although, I do not pretend to know that much about what goes on in Sombre's air as you know," she peered down at The Kestrel. "Is your transport in good order?"

"Always. It can't out-fly Spitfires though, Halliday. And definitely not half a dozen of them," he followed her eyes peering down grimly at his craft.

"Spitfires, oh ... no, I wouldn't think your little biplane could take those on. They're quite the zippy things aren't they," she said with a nod.

"Zippy is one way to describe them. 400 miles per hour is a hefty amount of zip. The engine in those things is as lofty as a war time brand gets - Rolls Royce."

32

"Yes," Halliday agreed looking a mite bewildered with the engine talk. She looked up as Recalcitrance Bexley stepped through the glass door with a fresh glass in her hand. Slender and darkly dressed in her flight jacket and leather pants, always sleek in her movement. She rolled her large bright eyes at them both. The drinking game was obviously over.

"So that was all quite a lot of macho stupidity that went on then. Dawdle' won," the aviatrix said as she pulled out a fresh cigarette from her case.

"Ah, yes but it had *you* entertained, didn't it woman," Halliday said with a twinkle in her eye, a knowing smirk.

"It was like watching two drunk baby-men. Quite the spectacle. I was actually hoping for a Mortdecai win." She gave an animated stretch, drink held skyward in her right, burning cigarette in her left. "So what are we all on about this evening?" She placed her drink down on a nearby table.

"Our Dave is being harassed, Recalcitrance," Halliday announced.

"Really? That *is* interesting. Do tell, Bi-Plane," she said puffing her smoke.

"I have some trouble coming from Strom-Pel. The Red Winged Death Command. Have you heard of them?" he queried the aviatrix.

She raised an eyebrow, "Not them in particular ... but Strom-Pel, Dave? Why in all of Sombre would you be drawing attention from there? That's fly-devil country." She let out another plume of smoke, "How exciting, eh?"

"Just a massive thrill, Miss Bexley, thank you." He said sarcastically then added, "They all fly Spitfires."

"Good god man!" she gazed down over at The Kestrel. "How do I say anything now that won't offend? As much as I admire the spit and polish you put into your little bird, it's not the most domineering of craft is it?"

Halliday cut in, "it is a nice flying machine, my Dave."

"But a flying bicycle compared to a Spitfire, Halliday Knight - you biased bugger," Recalcitrance smiled at her friend.

Dave didn't bite at Recalcitrance. Instead he sipped his ale and peered up at the skies.

It was a coincidence that he should just at that moment.

His well-tuned ears picked up the pitch of the well-tuned engines long before they came into view.

Downing the rest of his ale he nodded toward the threat coming in from the north sky. He announced rather glumly, "Well, they're here."

"Where?" Halliday said peering up. She searched the sky – for a good while. Finally she spotted them. "Oh, there. My word you've got a good set of ears on you, Dave Bi-Plane."

The six flyers closed in on the area in a rush; swooping in low, engines roaring. Blackened fuselages emitting blacker smoke, staining the air, the blood red wings of the Death Command shone venomously.

"Geez, yes, that is trouble, man," Recalcitrance said. "What do they want with you?"

"I don't know," he answered as they passed over The Ruptured Spleen and climbed the clouds like fire arrows.

It was only half a lie.

He wasn't entirely sure, but he thought he might know. "Yes, I have trouble."

34

CHAPTER 7
ON THE WAY TO THE BYWAY

Jasper woke and peered over at the clock. 2:54 am. He smiled. A break in his sleep, a well-timed pause. He still had over 4 hours left in Sombre. Dave Bi-Plane in trouble. Jasper Reeves to go back in.

Getting up, he light-footed across the hall and used the bathroom. He returned and slipped back under the covers, found the right spot on the pillow. With a satisfying rub of his toes on the sheets he waited. He knew his Rite of Passage nightmare was to come first; something he'd only woken up in the middle of a couple of times – when he had over eaten too close to bed. Scare factor eleven.

The darkness took over, he drifted away again.

D

The horde closed in. On foot, Jasper turned in circles, skateboard in hand, his only paltry weapon. It was all a nightmare, he knew it, but the threat was real. Silver teeth shone on each and every one of his pursuers. White caked, made up faces - black evil panda eyes. Fire torches clicked on and off - hissing gas flame. Metal bats were kept at sides. The males of the group were massive. The women all tall except one. And she was the speaker.

Her delivery was stoic, like verbal ice;

"Jasper Reeves, this is your unravelling. We're here for you and you only. Do what you can."

"Why me?" Jasper said.

She didn't answer, just let out a weird squeal that belied her natural tone from before. Like a whip, her chain struck his cheek bone hard, opening his skin.

Jasper swung his board, wild and pathetic, as he was set upon. An unreal blur of sneering evil panda faces and pain from machetes, metal bats, fire torches and chain lengths. The Arlington dark disappeared as the heaviest of blows smashed his forehead.

He went down.

Black.

Ɖ

"Well they must want something with you, Dave," Halliday said as she watched The Red Winged Death Command perform a series of barrel and dive rolls. "They are impressive at the sky tricks, aren't they."

"They know I'm here," Dave said with a heavy sigh. "How are they tracking me I wonder?"

"Sorry to go off topic, my Dave, but I might just sneak another of these in before I am called for a mission," Halliday shook her empty glass his way. "I shall go fetch. Would you like another?"

"No, I think I might just sit on this one," he looked down at the last third of his ale then continued to watch the command fly in formation. The black smoke from the Spitfire fuselages interested him. Did they run that hot?

"I'll have another, Halliday," Recalcitrance piped up lighting a skinny cigarette. "I am still here, you know, dangling away like a leprotic third leg."

"Ha! Oh sorry woman. Dave's aero fiasco is all dominating at the moment – you will have your spirit' in a jiff." Halliday said as she left them.

Recalcitrance stood next to Dave and followed his gaze. "Listen to those beautiful motors. The Spitfire is quite the plane, isn't it? So what have you done to peeve these flyers, Bi-Plane?" She blew a plume of smoke and rested her chin on her palm.

"Nothing directly," he said shaking his head. "I am going to have to find a way to take off from here though. I have just been given a mission. A Nightmarer in Brocken Ridge."

"Do you think they might try and shoot you from the sky?" the aviatrix said in the most matter of fact of tones. "They can go twice the speed you can."

"Try almost four times the speed," Dave said downing the last of his drink. He placed the empty glass on a nearby table, next to at least twenty other finished flutes, tumblers and shot glasses. He wondered who came and cleaned these up. He had never seen Orty leave the bar – a curiosity.

"Oh, are you leaving, my Dave?" Halliday said on her return. She handed Recalcitrance her Raspberry vodka.

"I must. I have a mission," he said with a heavy sigh. He gave the six planes in the sky a quick glance.

"I wish I could help you in some way," she said and touched him on the forearm.

He looked into Halliday's eyes. There had been plenty of times that he wished he could bring himself to say more to this woman. Right now was one of those times. The feelings were definitely there, bubbling away just below the surface. She gave him one of her warm smiles then took a sip of her beloved Scotch and Dry.

"I think I'll be fine. I am quite the flyer, you know," he finally said to them both. Halliday let her hand fall away. "Good evening to you all. Always a pleasure," he said giving both women a confident nod.

"Take care, Bi-Plane," Recalcitrance said then turned back round to watch his enemy circle the none too distant sky above.

He made his way back through the bar perplexed.

He knew he needed a plan.

He couldn't think of one.

D

Stepping through the elevator doors at the base of The Unexplained Mountain, Dave gave the skies a wary glance. He rubbed his hands through his leather gloves. They were hot. Not sweaty just yet. The sweat would come.

"Bastards of things," he muttered. Spitfires. Why did they have to fly Spitfires. The aircraft housed motors of beastly precision and timing. If there was any way to soup up The Kestrel, he would have done so by now. The engine housing only allowed the rotary motor. He had it ticking like a clock as well - but a ticking clock was hardly the roaring mechanism he needed to take on the likes of The Red Winged Death Command. "Hello Wilder - again," he patted Halliday's mare on her snout as he moved round her to get into the cockpit. The machanihorse gave her tail a whip and wandered off. He watched it go, massive metalized legs stretching her coat slightly at the joints. She snorted a puff of steam. He always thought Halliday Knight's transport quite the wonder.

At this moment he would have been happy to trade.

'Where is it Bi-Plane!'

He peered down at the small black-box radio. An addition he had made to The Kestrel's original controls – he had always thought it could use one. He felt like ripping it out and throwing it now. Could the Command' have tracked him through it somehow?

Enriching the mixture, he started the motor. Listening to the drumming of the rotary, he leant the mixture back to nine and flicked the switch to Copter mode. The plane shot up in its unconventional way, he levelled out and flew straight ahead with purpose – all he could do at present.

Knowing he had around two minutes left of Common Airspace before he reached the veritable safe haven of The Byway, he eyed his Vickers gun mount and realized he had no ammunition for the thing. It was a bloody ornament! What did he have to defend himself with? Two exaggerated pistols, a nine-inch blade and a lasso? Quite the pathetic list for air battle.

"Damn it all to hell!" he exclaimed as the sweat came.

The roar of Rolls Royce engines reduced The Kestrel's rotary to a timid sounding recreational, putt-putt as The Red Winged Death Command came to him: pulling up alongside, and in from behind, ahead at his front - surrounding him like a pack of air sharks.

'The gift, Bi-Plane! We've come for it!'

His blood froze. His suspicion was right. It really was the only thing he thought they could be after from him. Yet, to hear it spoken of out loud was something he thought would never happen. Secrets couldn't stay secrets forever it seemed. He was warned of this. Even as closely as he had guarded this one.

"Don't think so," he uttered under his breath - he wasn't about to engage in dialogue with anyone or anything from Strom-Pel. He eyed the greyed-out cabin window of the Spitfire at his right; the charred-black smoking fuselage, the stark contrast of the shining red wings. The machinations of the Spitfire engines actually shook the body of The Kestrel as he peered down at his gauges - airspeed reading at 92 mph, oil pressure was fine, he pumped more fuel. The Spitfire at his left clipped his top wing. He rode the bump.

'Now, Bi-Plane!'

The enemy at the right closed in to follow suit as Dave shot down dramatically in Copter mode – the only defense he could think of. With the sudden move he was at least a thousand feet below The Red Winged Death Command.

The Byway, the Gatherers astral gateway to all of Sombre presented, and he knew the Strom-Pel couldn't follow him in.

"Invite only here devils'," Dave said and pushed The Kestrel hard over 100 as the Death Command swooped screaming in a dramatic and desperate kamikaze-like dive. The Spitfires were fitted with the Jericho Trumpet, that unmistakable windy siren pierced his ears as the pilots opened fire from twin guns.

"Persistence is everything I guess," he muttered as The Byway swallowed Dave's Sopwith Camel amid a hail of flying bullets.

The Red Winged Death Command would never have known that bullets could never touch The Kestrel.

And neither would they have known that The Kestrel could never crash.

D

Dave breathed a lung-full of safe air and relaxed as he guided The Kestrel through Sombre's massive engine room.

Impossibly infinite, The Byway, the Gatherers most precious avenue into endless nightmare towns, boroughs and strangely concocted situations. The sky continually changed from sunlight's to nightfall's, from thunderous rainstorms to arid dry heat. Scenes flashed by with staccato-like quickness at the mighty walls. An eyesore of meshing colours : lightning flickered, storms crashed, humans and animals screamed and wailed – all a massive and endless caterwaul.

Yet, Dave Bi-Plane was grateful for it like he had never been. He spotted a Gatherer speeding along at the surface, a Speed Cycle rider, speeding through on toward a mission, waiting for entryway to present in The Byways wall. There was no way he could tell who the Gatherer was. There were quite a few Speed Cyclers.

As he awaited his own entry into the town of Brocken Ridge, his thoughts weren't for the Nightmarer that awaited his rescue. They were for his new enemies from Strom-Pel.

This Red Winged Death Command. Why here and why now bemused him to no end.

Yet now he knew what they were after.

The so called 'gift' they spoke of sat tucked just under The Kestrel's control panel, in a string tied brown leather pouch.

CHAPTER 8
MONOLYTH

It had been the third Dave Bi-Plane that had received it. Each and every time a new Dave Bi-Plane reached the inevitable end of his time in Sombre, the next Dave garnered his predecessors history, most of his thoughts and experiences – especially the important ones.

And this was definitely significant.

It had been on a rare break for *that* Dave Bi-Plane. For reasons unknown he had found himself in the town of endless tarmac, Loew Avion.

Loew Avion, a mass of interminable sky traffic flying endlessly toward the sun. Air balloons, blimps, jet fighters, helicopters, passenger planes, gargantuan air liners alike, all flew on and on. Quite a sight, but very much on the nonsensical side; just never-ending flight.

At least there wasn't *meant* to be an end.

It wasn't known whether its origins had started with drunken talk and story among Gatherers or elsewhere, yet there *was* a rumor, a historical wives tale for Sombre's mass of aviators, that if a pilot ever did make it to the end of Loew Avion, there would lie the town of Monolyth.

In Monolyth, a pilot would be granted immortality – a chance to live beyond their mere twelve strokes on their Beating Clock. To fly Sombre's skies forever.

Yet, it was just a tale. No aviator had ever been there.

Dave Bi-Plane had.

D

It hadn't happen exactly as all of Sombre's storytellers said it would.

The third Dave and The Kestrel had been flying alongside the throng of Loew Avion air traffic, slotted and uncomfortably dwarfed between a Boeing 747 and a gargantuan tourist dirigible, when the third Dave had heard a voice.

'I choose you, bi-wing flyer. Come down. I would like to enrich you. I have been waiting. I like you. I like your plane as well. Meet me in Monolyth.'

The voice was softly spoken yet rich with candor. It could have been a trick – but Dave didn't think it was. Without asking a "Who's that?" or saying as much as an "Okay, I will," Dave dropped The Kestrel down in copter mode.

He had never truly believed the stories. He was a smart man. Yet he wasn't one to buck if an opportunity presented, even as far flung as this one might have been. And he was sure the question would only be asked once.

Somewhere, half way between the air and the tarmac of Loew Avion, a chasm had opened for Dave and his Sopwith Camel. A hurricane-like wind rushed him down and inside. He landed the plane gently, motor cutting through the gold glowing ambience of the area where he had found himself. The sun so rich, it lit the trees and grasses, shone off the roof of the one small shanty house and turned the sandy pathway that led to the front door of the dwelling to gold dust. Honeycomb coloured cliffs rolled off into the distance guarding a crashing ocean. He'd killed the motor on The Kestrel and Monolyth's airy quiet filled his senses.

A longhaired fellow had stood in the doorway of the small dwelling. Dressed in a dark purple robe, he stood with hands down at his sides.

'Sir, please step down from your craft, won't you? This is the first and the only time I will do this.'

Dave obliged and walked toward the stranger. He wore a curled moustache and beard of an impressive length. He was also tall, at least a head and a half taller than Dave.

'Why am I here?' Dave asked. On closer inspection he noticed how luminous the fellow's eyes were, perfectly pinched ovals, a sparkling metallic green glaze in the pupils.

'So the rumor was true all along. This place does exist?'

'It does for now,' the fellow looked around Monolyth doubtfully as if he did indeed expected it all to just pick up and leave within a moment. Refocusing back on Dave, he held out his hand and Dave shook it.

On the exchange of greeting, he raised those eyes and grinned with rare warmth. 'I think I might have chosen well in you. Do you think I have chosen well?'

'Possibly. My name is Dave Bi-Plane.'

'And mine, sir, is McAdam Von Freign.' He dropped Dave's hand and studied him further, 'I am thinking it is indeed a pleasure to make your acquaintance. What luck. A good one.'

'What do you want with me? Are we still in Sombre,' Dave had said unnerved. If McAdam had a Beating Clock, he hadn't been able to see it.

'I cannot say no, and I cannot say yes. It is easier just to say this place is an existence. Neither magical nor completely without it. It is filled with hope though. My hope,' he bowed his head and shut his eyes. Opening them again he smiled, 'please stay where you are, in that very spot.'

McAdam turned and disappeared through the dark door way of his shanty house. There were sounds of rummaging through clutter. Dave listened to the ambience of Monolyth as he waited. The ocean crashing below sounded far more distant than it actually was. He had shut his eyes in search for clarity. He had decided that he wasn't in Sombre. There was no way Monolyth could have been. The stillness, the calm, was all an unimaginable mantra. Sombre didn't deal in places such as this.

He sensed that McAdam had returned and opened his eyes.

'Aha. Yes, Monolyth will do that for you ...' he'd stood watching Dave with a satisfied grin. He held something black and round in his hands.

'Dave Bi-Plane, for eons I have been watching the skies of Loew Avion. This is an auspicious occasion, one that is filling me with both uncertainty and wonder. I have finally settled and brought someone down from that sky. After our meeting, this place might just disappear forever, one can't always tell what will happen once a deed is done.'

McAdam held out his hands and presented Dave with a rough-cut blackened crystal. 'This is a protection charm of pure Thyst. It will protect you always.'

'In what way?' He held it in his palm. Although it was jagged, each edge had a smoothness. There was weight to it, yet it wasn't

*exactly heavy. He clasped it harder and there was a buzzing on his
skin. 'It's a tad odd isn't.'*

*McAdam had given him a satisfied smile as he pulled down on
his goatee. 'I expected honesty from you, and you haven't
disappointed me, airman. Indeed it does feel odd. Charmed things
always do. It should make you feel a little light headed as well if it is
doing its job properly.'*

*'What do I do with it? I have never owned anything quite like it.
What is its purpose?'*

*'Dave of the bi-wing flying machine, this is your protection.
Keep it safe on board your craft. Tell no one of its existence. Not a
soul. I cannot stress this enough. Respect. I think you have plenty of
this. You have it in spades and aces. Respect this charm and it will
always protect you while you are in the air. It must be kept safe and
kept secret from even your most trusted allies. Do this, and you and
your magnificent flying machine will always prosper in the air, will
always fly with Monolyth's embrace.'*

D

That was how it came about. A moment of complete
happenstance.

As he flew The Byway, Dave shook his head slowly. Strange,
strange, McAdam Von Freign. Whether Monolyth had indeed
disappeared after the exchange, Dave was sure he would never know.
Was the gift magical really? He wasn't sure of that at all. There was
one thing he did know though; The Kestrel hadn't crashed since. He
had lost his strokes from his Beating Clock, but he had always been
on foot – not while he was at the helm of his biplane.

Keeping true to his word, Dave had not and would not, breathe a word of its existence to a single soul.

So how did The Red Winged Death Command know he had it? The Byway opened in its customary way; with an ethereal yawning of new colour he had his entry to the town of Brocken Ridge. More than a little perplexed he guided The Kestrel left, and The Byway closed.

CHAPTER 9
DAY

Jasper rode to school knowing he was running late - he would have to get a pass from the office. Still a few streets away, he pushed the ground like a tired old guy. Attitude Adjustment's - *American Paranoia* album blasted away in his ears. (Truth known it was probably the only thing keeping him alert). His father boasted often that he had actually saw the band live at a club back in the day. Jasper was mighty jealous of this fact - the San Franciscan band were all sorts of awesome.

The night's adventure in Sombre had taken it out of him. All very active and enlightening. Dave Bi-Plane's plight getting more and more interesting upon each dream. The fact the man had a crystal of protection stashed away under the controls of The Kestrel was about as cool as it got. He wondered if he might guess what The Red Winged Death Command's actual deal was before Dave himself would? At the moment he hadn't a clue.

Sombre generally woke him up before his alarm; this sleep he woke with the clock still buzzing away like a malfunctioning door buzzer. Tensions were still high in the house as his mother was leaving for work. Jasper thought it had been best to stay in his room until she left; making him later. He was getting a little sick of stepping into the verbal crossfire between Tim and Julie Reeves. It was particularly nasty this morning. Threats were being thrown around the lounge by his mother as she rattled her keys.

'Look, I'm over it', 'I've had a-fucking-nough', 'I - we ... we just need a change is all, Tim, it's enough already!' - 'I'm going nuts here!'

What Jasper hadn't heard was nearly as much return fire from Tim Reeves. Once the front door had slammed shut, Jasper had waited an obligatory five minutes then walked out dressed and ready for school.

"Morning, dad. Running late. I'm just going to grab a bar and ten bucks from the jar if that's okay." He had said the words as nonchalantly as he could. From the corner of his eye he saw his dad sitting dejectedly.

"Morning, Jas'," he said in a tone about as limp as his posture in the wheelchair. He added, "Reckon we're going to move."

"Where?" Jasper had stopped in his tracks.

"Your mother has all the ideas, not me,' he said and turned to look out the window.

Feeling a little sick in the gut at the thought of a move, Jasper killed the music and kicked his board into his hands as he walked into the schoolgrounds.

D

He hadn't wanted to go home straight away after school.

Jasper dropped in on the bowl.

He ran a series of aerials as kids watched on.

Not that he even noticed them. He was in his own world; a world filled with Suicidal Tendencies blasting 'Trip at the Brain' and thoughts of his fracturing homelife. Friday. Trial day. D-Day for the Reeves. His thoughts darkened further - had it all become about the money for his mother? If it had, he thought it was pretty shitty of her. His father; *her* husband - sat slumped in a wheelchair on pain meds and probably anti-depressants and she was just after a filthy big pay cheque?

He finished his run and jumped from the bowl catching his board. Checking the wear on his wheels he walked to the bench where he had left his school bag and sat down for a spell.

"Those wheels are shanked, Jasper."

He looked up as a fellow skater he only knew as Emma rolled toward him and stopped. "Yeah, I know. Got another set at home. How's it going?"

"Fine and sunny, thanks. You look fairly grumpy, though," she said raising her eyebrows.

Emma was a short girl with small features, blue highlights through her blonde hair. She had a nice face and mouth, almond shaped eyes - high cheekbones; he thought her around his age.

"I mean, you always look sort of grumpy ..."

"Do I?" Jasper said a little taken aback.

"Yeah you do," she said and added, "but today you seem a bit too intense for your own good." Emma stepped off her board, flipped it up and leant on the tip.

"Lots of bullshit going down at home." Apparently, he was open to confide in this girl.

"The usual kind?"

"What's the usual kind?"

She rolled her eyes, "You know, the clichés – punchy mom or dad, drunk mom or dad, no mom or dad, stoned mom or dad ... a wicked stepmother that feeds you poisoned apples."

Jasper grinned, "that last one doesn't seem too likely."

"Made you smile at least," she sucked on her bottom lip. "Can I sit for a bit? My legs are sore. In between falls I've been pretty active today."

"Of course ... even though you called me grumpy," Jasper moved his bag to the concrete.

She sat down. "Well, let's face it. You aren't the most talkative among the crew that come to this park. In some ways that's good, because if you speak as much shit as some of the guys here, no one would ever know it."

"I keep to myself mostly," Jasper said stating the obvious.

Emma held the bridge of her nose, she shut her eyes, "Wait - about to sneeze ... shit - achoo!" She held up a hand pausing to see if there might be another. "Nup, all good. Dusty old park. Messes with my sinuses ... yes, you keep to yourself, we all know that, Jasper."

"I just found out that I might be moving away," he sat on his hands.

"Oh. Okay. Yeah right, that is tough. How long have you lived in Arlington?"

"All my life."

"Where are you heading off to? Bit of a shame, I'll miss watching you skate."

He spun what was left of his worn front wheels with his fingers, he could tell the bearings were still good. "No idea. Wherever my folks say I'm gonna go." Things fell silent.

He had decided share time was over. He wasn't about to allude to any more of his situation to Emma - his mother's continuous moaning, his father's therapy. The mere fact that a pending lawsuit could earn his already comfortable family an extra couple of million dollars wasn't great skatepark conversation. He knew some of the kids from around here had it tough, real tough.

"What are you listening to?" Emma said getting up, obviously sensing the discussion wasn't about to go much further.

"Excel. Crossover thrash band from the 80's." He smiled knowing she would have no idea who they were.

"Right, never heard of them. Enjoy." With a shrug, she tightened the windcheater around her waist and skated off, practicing a line. He watched her for a bit; she was fairly good – had good balance, kept good weight on her board.

He just realized then just how long it had been since he had a conversation with a girl his own age - as strained and cagey as that conversation was - as *he* had made it.

Emma was being nice – he wouldn't have blamed her for thinking him a bit of an asshole.

The bowl was empty. Turning his music back up, he got up for one last run.

D

The day wound up a little better than it started. After a tasty dinner of takeaway chicken avocado gnocchi, (a peace offering to his father from his mother for the way she left the house in the a.m.) Jasper sat at his desk and finished the 1000-word essay he had started the night before. It turned out to be one the best things he had written for a while. The first draft hadn't been as scratchy as he first thought, and once he started writing, the words just flew from his fingers. Hitting send on the email to his English teacher, he got up with a stretch and headed to the bathroom for a shower.

The water was hot therapy, he smiled as he thought of the airman's new plight - fending off The Red Winged Death Command. How in hell were they going to get Dave out of the sky? He'd just found out that Dave couldn't crash? The crystal he had been given by that weird mystic guy would always keep him safe if he just stayed in The Kestrel. That made sense. Dave rarely got out of the cockpit. He'd only lost strokes on his Beating Clock when he had been on foot - on missions when he absolutely had to spend a lot of time in a nightmare town and had been overcome by a citizen.

Dave Bi-Plane had 12 strokes - he had only lost 4, but the sense of loss Jasper felt waking after the airman perished bordered on real mourning. It was probably ridiculous to feel this way, but he did.

Such was his affinity.

It was an addiction. Whether it was good for him or not didn't matter. Sombre was magnificent. Sombre was an escape.

He needed it like breathing.

Turning off the taps, he reached for a towel. His conscience brought up another thing that needed to be dealt with - Emma from the skatepark. He regretted being like he was with her. Next time he saw her he would be nicer, instigate some conversation. What could it hurt? It wasn't like he was going to be around in Arlington much longer by the looks of things anyway. There would be no real tie - just a bit of friendly banter.

Entering his room he switched off all his lights and walked in the dark to his bed. Lifting the cover, he slid in snake-like and shut his eyes.

And waited.

CHAPTER 10
BURNING IN OLD SMOKE

Jasper had fallen asleep within ten minutes of lying down. His Rite of Passage into Sombre came charging, a subconscious window opening to dark ...

D

Early morning Arlington.

Rain had returned.

Jasper Reeves was a pathetic mess on the road.

His body had been cut in half; a machete slice straight through his gut. He was two pieces. His detached bottom half sitting cruelly and turned the wrong way; butt facing up. Feet hanging limply, having been broken and twisted 180 at the ankles.

The ten men and women stood watching, forming a guard. 20 black shiny boots on 20 black panted legs. He could see. He could breath. He wasn't dead? He wasn't even in pain – he felt light? Sitting up, resting on his hands he asked the question to any of them. "Why did you do this to me?" Apparently, he could speak as well.

"You were going to leave, Jasper. If you want to leave this town, you'll do it in bloody pieces."

They stepped back in unison and headed for the sidewalks as a roar of motors filled the streets of the town. Jasper turned and saw yellow headlights at the end of the road. Cars were coming. They didn't look they were about to stop for him either.

He screamed.

D

"O' this broken land is where we roam, forever in a soot filled home, we roam the falls of fire and dust, whatever will become of us.

We are the sodden chosen ones, the condemned forever woeful ones, we know the wretched world forgot us, the smoke we breath in woe begot us."

It was a young child that sung the haunting verse, in mournful acapella. A thin voice, whether male or female, Dave couldn't tell. As far as he knew, Old Smoke, was the only town in Sombre that had such a thing. A soundtrack to fit the landscape. The child sung it over and over.

In the distance, lights were on in contraption houses of seven and eight stories high. He hoped without hope that his Nightmarer would be in one of those. Leaving The Kestrel parked between a grey-bricked incinerator and a pile of burning rubbish (that had to be wet, he had noticed. It omitted far more smoke than fire), Dave had set out holding a handkerchief to his face with his left hand, making his way through the smolder and piping soot. The acridity of the area so dire it burnt through the nostrils and made the senses race – he needed to keep his senses. He carried his Exaggerated Pistol in his preferred right. He knew the place to be full of cunning chimney sweeps, desperate looters and loons - he didn't need a quick knife to the gut.

A minefield of fire pots shot up from the ground intermittently, and he changed his trajectory like a jogging drunkard. Making the ground even harder work was the earth-shaking rumble from chain and steam driven monster machinery.

Dave always wondered at the exceptional sleeping minds of the Nightmarers that conjured up such wild dreamscapes – wilder than one could ever imagine. He also wondered how Sombre went about snatching and trapping these dreams – it was an amazement. Suddenly he found himself amidst a flurry of steam machines, making him stop where he stood.

The singing child was drowned out by enormous, droning engines.

"Ho, ho, look out for us, man!" hollered a top-hatted driver haughtily through a bronze megaphone. He stood at the wheel working gears maniacally. The metal monster's movement was slow but pounding; it emanated extreme, filthy heat. Dave squinted and looked for a trace of his Nightmarer in its massive iron teeth. It was impossible to tell.

"Stop your machine now!" Dave pointed his pistol up at the driver as he ran alongside. "One shot is all it will take, trust me, fool!" The machine continued on.

"I said-!"

"You, Gatherer! Do you honestly think he can hear you?" Cutting him off mid-threat, a knife wielding woman jumped from the back of the machine. Goggles pushed up on her head, black hair dry as straw, her face was stained with grease - teeth surprisingly white. Her clock stroked high at 10 underneath her long carriage coat. He was a little taken aback at her speech. It was crisp, not a trace of the phlegm or cough in her tone – rare for Old Smoke.

"Well, climb back up that bleeding ladder and tell the bastard to stop, won't you!" Dave yelled at the woman over the metallic din. He coughed violently as he took in a throatful of the chronic air, "You know what I'm here for!"

"We haven't seen a Nightmarer! Try another Mononstarr Pinion Mouthed Carri-age', will you? There are plenty of them in

56

Old Smoke as I am sure you know!" She ran toward him animated, knife sticking out of her long sleeve.

He grinned and then burst into laughter, "Good lord, woman! What was that you called this machine?" His grip on his pistol eased. "Did you just say, Carri-age'?"

"Yes I did. What of it, Gatherer? Are you mocking it?" She cast him a murderous glare. "Have you ever been caught in its mouth? I am its technician. I know its power. I see the mess it makes first hand."

The bizarrely named Mononstarr Pinion Mouthed Carri-age', rolled on as the two continued their stand-off; long knife wielding technician facing an increasingly curious, Exaggerated Pistol toting Dave Bi-Plane.

"Your name please," Dave asked rubbing the stubble on his chin.

"Why would you want it?" She raised an eyebrow. "Gatherer's come and go through Old Smoke all the time. Seen thousands of your sort."

"There's nowhere near a thousand of us," Dave looked her straight in the eyes. This seemed to unnerve her.

"Well, plenty of you then. Why do you think my Beating Clock is at 10? You all kill without a clue in your head at times."

"You don't seem a typical Sombre citizen," Dave pocketed his pistol. "I'm not about to kill you, by the way."

"Fair enough. No, I'm not *typical,* as you put it." Sensing Dave was no threat she stuffed her blade back in her coat. She nodded, "Oh the driver, Willoughby, is a complete bag of nuts though. He chases hard and the Mononstarr eats. If any of you Gatherer types stopped to take the time you would see that the rest of us are just workers. Lowly. I'm the technician but still lowly; greasy, dirt-filled and blood-soaked. We have galley mouth cleaners for the Mononstarr, but even the technician must step in once in a while and help clean the giblets and edibles from the Mononstarr's chains."

She was quite the talker as it turned out.

"The name is Pen Raines. Not Penny – Pen. And since you have no interest in killing me, and so far, have been reasonable, I may as well know yours as well. This meeting will be fleeting as we both know, but I might run into you again before I go through my strokes."

"Dave Bi-Plane," he looked her up and down. She was shorter than he, quite light in build, wiry. "You are a technician? Both electrics and pneumatics?"

She nodded, "Both. And fuels - I need to be. The Mononstarr is a complex thing. Why do you ask, Dave Bi-Plane? Oh! Watch it!"

Bells clanged and both jumped sideways. A speeding tram car, fire box visible at the front shot spark and flame left and right as it past. Its whole undercarriage spewing fire as Dave watched it take on a corner hill then disappear over it.

"Whoa! That was rather close don't you think? That was that clod of all', Casey Daniels and his Fire Tram. Truth known he probably had your Nightmarer aboard. He's a mad opportunist that one. Beats Willoughby and the Mononstarr all the time to the troubled sleepers," Pen said not hiding her awe. She stood with her hands on her hips.

"Doesn't run on rails," Dave wondered aloud.

"Adds plenty of fumes to Old Smoke, though. Burns you as well if you get too close ... Oh well, Mr. Dave. I best let you get back to your business, wish you all the luck but I'll bet your Nightmarer's been swallowed by now. At least snuffled away where you won't find him or her."

Dave agreed. This had taken too long. But as it turned out, for this he was grateful. He watched her walk off in the direction the Mononstarr disappeared in.

Pen Raines seemed like a good thing to him. He needed someone like her. She was about to disappear in smoke. He hurried along, "Pen! Pen! Don't go just yet."

She stopped straight away; appearing to be in no rush to get back to her machine.

"Yes, Dave?" she turned and gave him a look that read both curiosity and concern. "What else could there be for this exchange? Have you changed your mind? Do you want to shoot me now? Are you Gatherers that bloody bloodthirsty? You need some sort of reward for your efforts however inane that reward might be?"

She talked a lot. But he could live with that for a while if he had to. It wasn't mindless gibberish she spoke; it was just a lot.

"Can you let me get a word in please Pen?"

She stood with her arms folded. "Okay then, but I need to get back to the Mononstarr."

"How about if you didn't go back?"

"What do you mean?"

"I mean, leave Old Smoke and come with me. I need an assistant. I think you would fit the bill rather well."

Pen Raines didn't answer straight away. She just stared - he tried reading the grimace on her small face. He hoped for a quick sell. It didn't look like he was going to get one. "Surely a change of scenery wouldn't go astray. All this smoke, Pen ... I'm offering you a break from it."

"To do what, exactly?"

"Come fly with me in my Sopwith Camel. I need a technically minded individual like you. You look light for the trip as well. I could really use the help." He realized he was gesturing a lot with his hands, something he didn't do often – he was coming off needy but didn't care.

"The Mononstarr needs me though ... like I've already told you a dozen times already, I am its technician."

She was prone to exaggeration - they hadn't even been talking long enough for her to mention it a dozen times. He gave her a hopeful look,

"Have you ever wondered what the rest of Sombre looks like? I can show you."

Ideas were popping in his head like soap bubbles. This would be the best way to fight The Red Winged Death Command – a two-pronged attack, straight from The Kestrel. He hadn't come here looking for an assistant, a Pen Raines – now he wasn't about to leave without her.

"I must admit, I *have* wondered. I only get a glimpse when I'm getting rebuilt at The Office of The Menders. There are all-sorts there," Pen said shifting her weight onto her left.

"This is all a bit much to take in," she rubbed her temples. "Flying. Would Sombre even allow me to leave?" She grinned to herself, "It would be nice not to have to listen to this damned child sing this irksome song anymore. I generally do well and can ignore it. But at times ... Dave Bi-Plane, can you tell if it is a boy or a girl singer?"

60

Pen Raines would make for good company. He smiled as he was made aware of the verse again – he really couldn't tell, "No, I can't. What is your answer? Do I have an accomplice? If so, we best be going."

She brightened, "You know, I think I will. Why not? You seem a likely type, Dave Bi-Plane. I think you will treat me well. Will you? Willoughby can be quite the headstrong tyrant at times – just because one can steer a machine in a straight-line and operate an extremely simple and perfunctory metal jaw, does not make one god, now does it? Takes my own bleeding brilliance for granted as well."

Brilliance. Whether she was exaggerating again or not, it sounded good to Dave. He needed some brilliance.

The two walked back in the general direction of where Dave thought he arrived. "This acrid smoke, Pen! How in Sombre have you put up with it for so long?"

"And that bloody singing child as well!" Pen Raines said loudly, "will not be missing that one. Think I have heard that song at least 3 billion times over."

3 billion, Dave doubted that.

Pen Raines was prone to exaggeration.

CHAPTER 11
COMBATANTS DEUX

The conversation had been rather one sided on the way back to The Kestrel. Pen Raines, a wealth of information on coppers and steam, metal and electrical wiring. The Mononstarr Pinion Mouthed Carri-age' was indeed quite the amazing machine. The general upkeep and complexities of its structure would have indeed kept her busy. There were three others of its kind in Old Smoke as well.

"The competition for Nightmarers around here is quite high, Dave." She gestured ahead, "Oh look, there's another hunter - a Limberial Insizor. All jaw, aren't they? There are six of those ..."

Dave stopped.

Her nonchalance belied the machines appearance entirely. "What sort of motor is in that thing? Good god! It sounds like its grinding metal on metal." Dave stood in awe. The Limberial Insizor was nowhere near as large as the Mononstarr. The driver was nowhere near of the same kind as Willoughby either. Pale and fat, drenched in sweat, the bald man wore a dirty singlet top and black, ill-fitting trousers. He stood on a long metal tray, scowling and looking distraught as he operating an assortment of levers that kept the machine in a straight line.

"You know when you can just look at something and feel the pain it could inflict on you?" Pen said in wonder.

Indeed, the Limberial Insizor had a massive trap-like chrome jaw of pointed blades - the bizarre machine jogged along at a hunting pace, pistons fizzing on its six scissoring, iron legs. Dave squatted down and searched its undercarriage; there were all sorts of moving parts to pull a Nightmarers body through the machine once trapped and swallowed by that jaw.

Like the heaviest of metallic steaming insects, it continued off into the smoke.

"That is one of the wildest things I have seen for some time," he said clearing his throat.

"Yes, one not to get in the way of. That driver, Fat Stanton, he'll never master it properly. He's toppled over the front into its jaws on more than one occasion," Pen nodded.

The two continued walking the cobbled road and finally, Dave spotted The Kestrel, looking about as meek as anything could compared to the monster machinery he had just witnessed in Old Smoke.

"This will be a change for you, Pen Raines," he said as he picked up his pace. The two crossed the way and approached his aircraft.

"I have never flown, Dave," she said rubbing her nose. "Are you a solid pilot?"

"Better than some," he smirked at her gall as he patted The Kestrel on its tin fuselage. "Here," he webbed his hands ready to give her a boost up.

"Thank you, Dave. I already have about one thousand thoughts on how we could improve this machine," she lifted her foot, put one hand on his shoulder and the other on The Kestrel. She was hoisted up.

"Well, I will be glad to hear them, Pen," he said then muttered under his breath, " ... all one thousand' of them."

Dave hopped into the cockpit and turned to face his co-pilot. "There should be a helmet in there somewhere. You already have goggles ... I'm not used to having an extra aboard my transport."

"Well, I am keen and willing, Dave Bi-Plane," Pen pulled out the helmet and looked at it curiously, she eyed the inside and gave it a wipe. "You say you have been generally solo as a Gatherer. Why do you need me suddenly? You haven't really said."

"Hmm ... Yes, I have chosen to omit the real reason I have offered you a role, haven't I?" Dave scratched his chin.

"Thus far," Pen said as she tried her helmet on. "This is a reasonable fit - it didn't look like it would be."

He thought the helmet looked a tad strange on, but he wasn't about to allude to it. "Well, maybe I was hoping you wouldn't back out."

She pursed her lips and raised her brow, "Why? How bad is it?"

He wasn't about to start the engine until he told her. Sure that starting The Kestrel would come off like the slam of a coffin lid on her fate.

"Oh, you'll be quite safe while you're aboard this aircraft. And whether you get out of your seat when I am called on a mission will be entirely your prerogative." He sighed as he listened to the child sing its mournful verse for what would be the last time.

"Understood, Dave. Continue," she fiddled with the tie strap under her small chin.

"But I have to confess that there is a specific task that I need your help with. I need you to help me fight, Pen. A fight that will be too much to tackle on my own."

"Right ..." she stopped with the tie strap and looked up, "who is it that we'll be fighting, Dave Bi-Plane?"

"The Red Winged Death Command."

He held his breath for a moment imagining the very sound of the name would send a chill through to her core.

"Alright ... and who are they?" she nodded continuing to work on the strap, "This tie strap is incredibly fiddly, Dave. I reckon I could come up with about one hundred better fasteners than this one ..."

Heartened by her reaction he continued. "Pen, we will be facing six Spitfire planes from Strom-Pel, all with V12 motors and a cruising speed twice as fast as our fastest."

"So we'll have to work towards getting faster," she shrugged.

"They will shoot at us."

"We'll have to shoot back then."

"We don't have the guns," he shook his head slowly.

"Then we'll get them – or I'll make them - one or the other."

"This could cost you another stroke on your Beating Clock. Be sure that you are at ease with that. I don't want to force you to do any -"

"Enough please, Dave!" Pen threw her hands in the air. "Did you want me to come or not?"

"Well, yes I do," he said. A grin formed on his lips.

He had his technician.

"Then I suggest you get this bird into the sky then."

She sat with folded arms and waited.

"The Kestrel," he said and started the engine.

"Yes, a bird, Dave," Pen said and smiled.

D

Dave pushed The Kestrel hard and high, out of the dark grey congestion of Old Smoke and into Sombre's great Common Airspace. Clean and breathable air swept the senses. The skies were clear with a red sunset forming in the west. Sombre had chosen it to be dusk at this very moment. He knew there to be no particular time in Sombre. No standard day or night. Any real-world conventional time be damned.

"Ha! This is will do me nicely, Dave." Pen attempted to break into his thoughts as she laughed into her radio from the backseat.

"What?"

"I said this will do me nicely!" she yelled.

"Sorry, again?"

"This is wonderful, Dave!" she gave a final belt from the back.

"Oh. Oh yes!" Dave agreed. "You'll have to speak up."

"This radio of yours is a box of rubbish, Dave!"

"Hold on," he smiled as he dropped The Kestrel into a quick barrel roll. The skies span round and round as he performed the elementary stunt.

"Whoa! You *can* fly! Can I have a bit more warning in future, though? I shall need to brace myself for that type of thing! My head's all soupy!"

He smirked. There would be no promises there. "Okay!"

"Where are we headed, Dave?"

"I thought it would be best to get back to my garage. Get you acclimatized to your new situation," he yelled.

A familiar heavy roar of engines sounded above.

'This cannot be avoided, Bi-Plane. This is your fate! Surrender the gift!'

"My god! Where did they come from?" he said and looked up. A few hundred feet above The Kestrel, The Red Winged Death Command appeared in formation.

"Is that the enemy, Dave?" Pen yelled.

"Indeed it is. There is to be no respite it appears. They are a bug on my backside, Pen."

"Dave, those motors are huge! I can hear the work in them!" she piped in awe. "This is massive trouble for us!"

"I know that, Pen!" he said then evened his pitch in an effort for calm. "If they shoot, they will miss, I know it. We just need to try and get this plane to the palace."

"How far is this palace?" Pen said doubtfully as the 'Death Command quickly broke formation and peeled off into a rolling descent, Jericho Trumpets wailing like crazed banshees.

Dave accelerated, pushing his small plane to its limits. A staccato string of close Browning machine gun fire came at The Kestrel. Every shot missing his craft as expected. Each bullet failing to hit his head and shoulders by mere inches.

"No!" He had a sudden gut-wrenching realization. Could she? He chanced a quick look over his shoulder.

"Get down, Pen! Get way down in your seat!"

If there was an answer from his new co-pilot, he wouldn't have been able to hear it as The Red Winged Death Command had enveloped The Kestrel's airspace. A massive roar of Rolls Royce motors drowning out all other sound. Dave Bi-Plane's world was all blood red wings and burning black fuselage. Four of the Spitfires had him surrounded.

He was sure he could detect more threats in his radio, but it was impossible to hear them. The machine gunfire continued from behind. "Pen!"

The girl hadn't heard a word he had said; and as fate would have it, it happened as Dave had turned around to check. Flaming-yellow, Browning gun fire cannoned in from close proximity. Pen Raines writhed in her seat - bullets riddling her back and shoulders. Blood sprayed in release as her head exploded at her neck.

He had told her she would be safe!

"Jesus! You bastards!" Dave gasped helplessly as the high spires and black glass of the Steppanaire air palace appeared in a rush.

Deed done; The Red Winged Death Command filed off with a last warning;

'There will be more, Bi-Plane! Surrender the gift!'

D

Jasper woke with a jolt.

His eyes were wet. Had he been crying?

CHAPTER 12
WORLD FIRSTS

Jasper stood blinking in the bathroom mirror, tooth brush protruding from his mouth.

His skin had a yellow tinge - like light bruising at his cheekbones. He wasn't seeing things. He was sure of it.

His mother and father couldn't see it though. He had asked them at breakfast. Both studied his face curiously and said no - then gave each other a glance. (There seemed to be some kind of joint resolve between them this morning which was a relief.)

The yellow was definitely there though. Why only he could see it was odd. Was he getting sick?

Last night's Sombre experience was about as eventful as it got. But he hadn't woken jubilant like usual - he was exhausted, and his neck and shoulders were sore. Wet eyes generally meant crying as well. Dave had met Pen Raines and was sort of responsible for having her killed straight away. Had that upset him that much?

With a rinse and a tap he dropped his tooth brush into the holder. Taking a last look at his sickly complexion he left for school.

D

Arlington's weather had been hit and miss all day; as if some sort of indecisive god of earthly conditions couldn't decide if it wanted to smile sunlight or cry rain.

Jasper had decided to still go to the skatepark after school. He knew the bowl would be dry enough, and he didn't have much homework - just an easy social studies quiz.

He pushed the gate open and rolled toward the large bowl, noted a few kids on scooters over at the small bowl; a couple of new skaters practicing street. 'Crush the Demoniac' by the Cro-Mags blasted in his ears in all its metallic-hardcore-crossover-fury. He grinned. The track was the perfect mix of aggression and melody - mixed attitudes – suited his state of mind perfectly.

Throwing his bag under a bench seat he pushed off, dropped in and proceeded to thrash out a series of aerials. There was instant release. He breathed. A skate, just what he needed to shrug off the weirdness of the day.

He saw the yellow in his face again in the bathroom mirror at school. What in the hell was that about?

He slashed the coping and dropped back in.

Only he could see it. No one gave him a funny look in the halls at all. He had felt off all day though. Not really sick. Just, off.

He pumped hard, ran the long side of the bowl, leant back, hit a 360, landed it and grinned.

A night of Sombre and Dave Bi-Plane had never left him this way. It was always fist pump worthy, never melancholy, never weird-yellow-face inducing ...

He pumped hard, and launched, grabbed the nose and backside aired. Tiring, he dropped to faky at the far end and slid to a stop. He needed his water bottle. He walked and jumped up on the coping and hoisted to the flat.

"You should wear a helmet once in a while, you know."

He looked round in the direction of the familiar female voice. It was the girl, Emma, watching him again.

"It was good viewing, though. You're definitely the best around here, Jasper."

70

"Yeah, right ... there's plenty of others," he blinked as he looked her way. Emma sat on her board; long white Santa Cruz t-shirt and baggy black shorts. He pulled out his water bottle and gulped. Killing his music, he rolled over to her - she was nice enough. He may as well be sociable - given how much of an ass he was last time they met.

"I see you changed your wheels over - oh! Oh, frig! Jasper?" she exclaimed.

"What?" he said as he sat down on his board and looked her square in the eyes.

Her wide eyes.

He saw it straight away.

Emma had the same yellow on her cheeks.

D

For what seemed like an eternity they could both only sit and stare at each other. As if one was waiting for the other to burst into flames.

Emma was the first to speak. "What does this mean, Jasper? I thought it was just me. We barely know each other." She touched her cheeks with her finger tips.

"I know. I had it as soon as I woke up this morning," Jasper said. He shook his head slowly. "Has anyone commented at all? Could they see it?"

"No."

"Same."

An awkward silence settled in between them. Jasper had no idea what to say next.

Emma spoke instead. "Jasper, do you go there?"

"Where?" He said knowing she could only mean one thing.

She raised her brow, "I think you know where." She pointed to her face – then his. "This is all it could possibly mean. When you sleep. Where do you go? You said you were yellow when you woke up this morning. So was I."

Her eyes lit up. "You go to Sombre as well, don't you! Who do you become?"

Holding his breath, he bit into the inside of his mouth. Was he about to speak out loud to someone about his Nightmare world? Sombre? Was he? As surreal an idea as it was - he was.

He kept his tone low, "Dave Bi-Plane ... I fly a biplane."

Shocking him greatly, Emma pushed off her skateboard onto her knees and threw her arms around him.

"Shit, Jasper! Sorry I have to hug you to make sure you're real! This is too weird! I'm Pen! Pen Raines, the tech from Old Smoke! The girl in the coat and the dry hair!"

The unexpected affection felt surprisingly good. How long had it been since he had embraced someone? He hugged back with one hand at her shoulder. The moment ended, they both sat back down on their boards. Emma was beaming.

"Pen Raines flew with your Dave last night, didn't she!" She said shaking her head slowly. "I can't believe this."

"Either can I," Jasper agreed then added, "it didn't end well though did it. Pretty sure her head exploded."

"I know. I think my days, well nights ... whatever you want to call them, in Sombre are numbered." She rubbed her thumbs on her grip tape, "This has to be some sort of a sign though, doesn't it?"

"I guess so," he shrugged not feeling entirely sure about this new development. As strange as it sounded, it had only been he and Dave for so long. Was Emma and Pen a wanted intrusion? He wasn't so sure.

"Thinking your Dave Bi-Plane is a bit of a one in a million-man, Jasper," she gave him a wink and giggled, rubbing the stud at her ear lobe. "Pen is a little taken with him, I think. Ha!"

"Hmm ..."

Jasper thought it best to steer the discussion away from any kind of romantic line between the two. He stared directly at the pale yellow in Emma's face. It was absolutely there. This wasn't coincidental at all. An absolute shot from a stratosphere unknown to anyone but he and Emma.

"What's your surname, Emma?"

"Cartwright. Yours?"

"Reeves."

"What school do you go to. Haven't seen you at Massa'."

"Because I don't go there. I go to WhiteHill."

"Seriously? That private girls school?"

"Yes, Jasper. And what about that?" she challenged raising her eyes, adding coolly. "My mother is the vice principal."

He held up his hands, "Hey, no judgement here. You are who you are, Emma." He grinned and laughed, "You skate, you dream of Sombre. You're cool."

"I'm in Sombre at the *moment,*" she reminded him, "Not sure how long Pen has left. One stroke. It will all depend on your Dave Bi-Plane by the looks ... no pressure, Jasper."

He nodded. "I'm surprised she went with Dave actually. He's in a fair bit of trouble right now."

"Obviously. That squad of planes are super scary."

"The Red Winged Death Command."

"Cool name," she stared down at the concrete. "Woke up with a chronic sore neck and head this morning from that wild decapitation. Not the worst I've felt from a night of Sombre and Pen Raines, though. Used to get wild acne in the early days. I would always wake up coughing - had to drink a gallon of water. Vomited a couple of times. Old Smoke is a shocker." She looked up. "How do you wake up after being Dave Bi-Plane?"

"Okay. Pretty good usually. Although, this morning was rough. I think Dave felt responsible for Pen getting shot up," he added, "he's in his plane a lot. He's good at his job."

"Sounds like you've had a whale of a time with it, Jasper Reeves. I have to admit that it's been tough being Pen. This Dave Bi-Plane thing is a welcome change for her," she said and pulled out a pouch of tobacco and a cigarette paper. "As long as your Dave can keep her safe long enough so she can enjoy it. Shame this didn't happen a little earlier, when she still had plenty of strokes left on her Beating Clock."

He watched her fill the paper with tobacco, lick the edge and roll it with her small fingers. She struck a match and lit up.

"Oh. Would you like one, Jasper? Sorry. I just thought you didn't look the type."

"I'm not. I'm good, thanks," he said awkwardly and looked the other way. A skater. Private school. A smoker. He knew nothing about this girl.

She smirked and nodded, "Just like one occasionally, particularly while I'm chatting. *Particularly* chatting on out-of-the-fucking-blue life changing events such as this."

74

She blew a plume of smoke and gave him a slightly pensive look. "I remember last time we met you mentioned you will be moving away. That still happening?"

"I think it might be. It's mom's idea. When she makes up her mind, she usually gets her way." He divulged further. "Dad had an accident. He's in a wheelchair, he's in rehab and stuff ... it's all just been complicated and shit really," he trailed off.

Emma exhaled another mouthful of smoke. "Doesn't sound too good. That's pretty big Jasper. When stuff like that happens, it *should* cause some sort of upheaval." She huffed, "It does beg the question though, doesn't it?"

"What does?"

"Well, I've seen you at this park about a thousand times over the last couple of years. We've never really spoke, just a nod while you blast your senses with your old school thrash punk ..."

"Did you do some homework, Emma?" he grinned.

"I did look up that band Excel – had a listen. Not so bad. They do a 'Police' cover. Pretty cool," she said and stubbed her cigarette out on the concrete.

He gave her an appreciative nod.

"But you know, if this is Sombre's doing, why would it choose now to give us this yellow bruised face so we could see each other? Why make Pen meet Dave Bi-Plane? Pen can't be long for Sombre, which I would imagine, means either am I. Puzzling isn't it?"

Jasper shrugged his shoulders, and added completely zilch to the conversation, "I guess. I've got nothing."

She gave him a searching look, "It all just seems to be drawing to an end when it's sort of only the beginning. Shame, huh?"

"Can't wait to see what happens tonight though," Jasper said brightly not sure if it was the right thing to say, as Emma seemed to be having a down moment. She had talked herself into the doldrums. Girls seemed to do that a quite a lot he thought.

With a sigh she picked herself up off her board. "I don't love endings Jasper. Only beginnings. Do you appreciate what we have here at all? This is beyond rare, and it already has a time limit."

Shaking her head, straight mouthed, she pushed off slowly and ended the conversation with a dejected, "It sucks. See you later."

CHAPTER 13
THE TOLL

"It's been nice knowing you all, Jasper. Take it easy won't you." A teary-eyed Cathy the therapist, carried her bag over her shoulder, leaving the Reeves household for the last time it seemed. "I've been let go."

"Oh, okay ... by, sorry." He mumbled. She passed by him with a sharp flick of her blond hair.

"Yep," she said with a huff walking the short path to the gate. She clicked it open and spoke her final words, "struggling to pay my fucking bills as it is, is' all."

Jasper knew it was one more nail in the Arlington coffin.

D

Laptop open at the lounge table; Tim Reeves was scrolling a real estate site as Jasper crossed through on his way to his bedroom.

"Hey dad. Cathy gone, eh," Jasper said and added, "she's fairly pissed."

"I know," he answered without looking up. "Had to be done sooner or later. Was never going to be nice – she works for herself."

"Right," he shrugged, "Call me when dinner's ready. I've got some homework to do."

"You wanna know where we'll probably end up when we move?"

"Not really. I'll have to go along with it anyway," he answered shutting his door. He heard his father call out, "Jas', don't be like that, man."

He chose to ignore him. It wasn't that he was *that* angry about the impending move, maybe a little dejected. He just had no say in it. He was to be the related tagalong. Whatever the town, he just hoped it would have a reasonable skatepark. Deciding he needed to hear some old punk on vinyl, he headed straight for his LP collection. He flicked through and pulled out his copy of Black Flag's 'Damaged'. A classic straight from his father's original hand-me-down's - the sleeve was worn and creased up on the corners - he smelt the age as he pulled out the vinyl. Awesome. Slipping it out with care, he placed it on the turntable, watched it spin as the needle hit the grooves. Edgy punk guitar introduced a savage Henry Rollins as he spat out the words to 'Rise Above'. Shutting his eyes, he nodded his head along to the track as he made his way back to his bed and lay down.

He thought of Emma Cartwright of the skatepark - Pen Raines of Sombre. Why on earth was he being introduced to her this way? Sombre felt so real to him at times that he may as well be flying Dave Bi-Plane's Sopwith Camel himself. But this? She was right - it was beyond rare. The timing was so odd though. An otherworldly joining of dream compatriots that didn't really make any sense in real life. He was on his way out, and so was she, just in another way.

"Strange," he muttered.

Black Flag's savage punk rock fueled the dissonance.

D

Store bought Butter Chicken and judicial talk. Dinner had been filled with cross referencing details on Fridays pending settlement hearing. The whole thing was a lock. Jasper had been tuning in and out of the discussion as he chewed. There would be no case. Only his father, shadowed by his mother, sitting down with some smarmy lawyer to hear about the payout the Reeves's would rake in from Mistral Foods.

It sounded like both his parents wouldn't have to work for a while.

"I tried to show Jas where we'll probably be moving to ... wasn't interested," his father announced.

"Don't care," Jasper said petulantly.

Placing her fork down, Julie Reeves wiped her mouth with a napkin. "That's okay, Jasper. I would rather not announce anything until after Friday. After Friday, we'll expect you to be on board though. This is for your father first, and you and I last. You do get that don't you?"

"And the money. It's a lot about that isn't it," Jasper said shaking his head. He went to get up from the table. He'd had enough food and more than enough of this discussion.

"Are you saying I'm a shallow money grabber? I hope that isn't what you're saying Jasper," his mother's eyes lit up, she warned, "You wouldn't want to be."

Jasper looked to his father, he appeared concerned as the exchange elevated, but at the same time, as meek as hell. Disappointing.

"You know the amount of shit your father has been through since the accident. The whole thing has been rough ... if we need some compensation for the upheaval of our lives, we're damn well going to get it!" She poured more wine in her glass and made a fist in frustration. "Do you think I'm about to go down to H+M and blow the lot on fucking dresses? Go buy a new Audi? Is that what you think? Do you think so little of me, Jas'? Do you?"

The question was left unanswered. A tear ran down her cheek and she dabbed it with a napkin. The room was deathly silent.

"I -"

He was completely clueless as to how to continue. The last time she had let loose like this at him was when he was 13; when he got a ride home from the park in a stolen car. The car crashed into a wall; the driver was an older skater who knocked himself out when the air bag set off. The crash broke the nose of the other passenger - Jasper's last proper friend in Arlington, Davey 'Doc' Holliss. The cops were called. The car was searched later, and a bag of coke had been found in the glovebox. Davey threw Jasper's name up straight away, even though he was only in the car for five minutes. It was massive at the time. He hadn't forgotten it neither. And he hadn't forgotten the scolding from his mother. Tim Reeves had to try and keep her calm. On second thoughts, maybe she wasn't as mad as then. But he had cut her pretty bad.

"Sorry, mom."

"Can you go someplace else, Jasper. Anywhere else." She took another sip of her wine.

"Better go, Jas,'" his father reached for his mother's arm and gave it a rub.

He studied his parents eyes. There was something else going on here that he didn't understand that was for sure.

He left without another word.

D

Accompanied by solid early 80's crossover thrash from a playlist painstakingly compiled over the past three years; Jasper folded the homework quiz over and stuffed it into his schoolbag. He stretched and yawned, killed the music and prepared himself for another night of Sombre and one Dave Bi-Plane. Dave Bi-Plane with a twist it had to be said. It all felt heavier – the lead weight of the wellbeing of Pen Raines and Emma Cartwright. After a fast brush of his teeth he crossed the hall to his room and stopped midway – the house was black - his folks had retired for the night. He found their sudden unity disconcerting for some reason, which he knew was stupid.

"Whatever ..." he huffed and entered his room. Clicking the door shut he turned off the light, walked to his bed in darkness.

"Let's go, " he uttered and shut his eyes tight.

D

As Jasper slipped away, his Rite of Passage nightmare continued ... a savage early morning on the streets of Arlington.

The last of the headlights disappeared in the distance.

He had been ran over again and again.

He was mere roadkill; a flattened obliterated ribcage, legs and backside a ribbon-like jellied mess of skin, denim and blood.

Cruelly, he seemed to be still alive. The dream state allowed such things. His assailants continued to watch him from each side of the road; 5 on his left, 5 on the right. All motionless.

"Hey! What'n fa' fuck ith' thith?" He spoke through a wildly malformed mouth, his tongue feeling too fat to fit in. He was livid. Pathetically so. Just a gory mess on the street.

"We're going to let you move on, Jasper Reeves." It was the familiar female voice again. She spoke calmly from the left side of the road. Stepping from the curb, she walked, metal bootsteps tapping on the wet tar, "It was never going to be easy for you. Its harsh and final. And a complete pain in your ass, I'll bet." Suddenly her face was up close, looking at him straight in the eyes. Those chrome teeth luminous in a broad grin; white eyes glowing in the greasy black panda makeup – despite the disguise, the features were unmistakable. It was his mother.

"It's all a bitch, isn't it, Jasper."

Another motor roared into life as headlights appeared once again. The car braked mere feet from his body. The engine revved and grunted like a pissed off bull.

There was a scraping under his head as it was lifted ...

CHAPTER 14
KEEPING PEN

Pen Raines seemed very small as she recovered on the chrome table at The Office of The Menders. Dave Bi-Plane stared down at the not yet conscious girl in wonder. Her head completely rebuilt, her features were small and clean, chin pointy but too pointy - topped with black hair, strands that were still needle straight, but nowhere near as smoky and straw-like as when they had first met. The Menders did great work.

The Old Smoke technician had an innocence that he hadn't picked up on at first. Her black knee length coat was open exposing her Beating Clock - now stroking at eleven. He shook his head slowly.

"So what have you decided, Dave? I wouldn't say this *isn't* a cruel way for her to finish her time in Sombre." Hamish the Mender stood at his shoulder. He appeared surprisingly fresh faced, dark hair in good order. Dave always wondered how the man ever got any down time.

"Look I know," Dave sighed still shaking his head.

"I mean there is nothing saying you can't do it, but Pen Raines will float in The River once she is through her strokes. She isn't special, she isn't a Gatherer. She won't live on through another Nightmarer." He sighed. "Quite frankly, Dave, this seems a little out of character for you."

Dave tapped his upper lip in contemplation. Hamish was right of course. The man was making sense as always. "As I explained when I brought her in, I needed her help, Hamish. The Red Winged Death Command are far too much for me to take on alone. The machine she worked on in Old Smoke was impressive. Her technical knowledge is far greater than my own. I was hoping she could give me advancements that could help me fight back." He looked down his brow at Hamish and added defensively, "She did want to come you know."

"The Red Winged Death Command. They fly Spitfires, don't they? Any idea why they're after you, Dave? Aren't they from Strom-Pel?" Hamish frowned appearing to already know the answer.

"They are."

"That's a part of Sombre we can't get The Funneling into you know. I'm not even sure it is actually part of Sombre. This office has never been there, but I have heard enough over the eons, and there would be nothing solid to lay its foundation. It's just atmosphere."

"Evil air," Dave said and nodded.

"Yes, nothing good."

Pen Raines opened her eyes.

"Ah. She wakes," Hamish said and moved to the bench. He leant over the technician. "Don't move just yet, Pen. I just need to check your vitals and senses."

Dave continued on as he watched Hamish check Pen over, "They'll never shoot me down, but they could force me down ... they are well skilled, not to mention twice the size of my Sopwith."

"But still, you know I'm right. If *you* had only one stroke left, how would you want to use it?"

There was a grumbling from the bench.

"Shush, Pen. Just a few extra checks then you can talk all you want. You've had a complete rebuild of your cranium using some

84

reanimated parts. I need to ensure they all work." Hamish held her head gently and tilted it slightly right, lifting the chin.

Dave watched on motionless as he pondered the outcome of all this. He was solely responsible. She would have to go back. It was the only moral thing to do.

"You didn't answer my question in its entirety, Dave Bi-Plane. Why are these Strom-Pel Flyers after you?" Hamish said as he scraped a thin metal instrument around the insides of Pen's eyes.

"Oh my god, man! That looks like it would smart!" Dave squinted.

"The cavities are still numb, Dave ... don't change the subject! Why are they after you?" Hamish shook his head and sucked in through his teeth.

Dave lied with variety, "It could be a whole host of reasons. The Sopwith,' a Gatherer grudge, a want to convert me to a Strom-Pel pilot. I am the only true Gatherer plane pilot after all. I really don't know, Hamish, but they definitely have a bug in their backside."

"Hmm. That all sounded like a bunch of gloss – as per usual," Hamish sighed, "anyway, she is brand new – and on stroke *11*. Do what you decide. I know what I would do." He turned and gave Dave a grim look and left the two alone.

D

The Funneling opened onto the black polished glass of Sebastien Steppanaire's air palace. An arguing, Dave and Pen stepped out of its brilliantly lit opening and with a warping shimmer it was gone.

"Pen, you know I want you here. But what an absolute pig of a man I would be if I was solely responsible for your demise! Your actual demise!" Dave said loudly.

Pen's arms were tucked tightly, she was livid,

"And I said I would rather stay on, Dave Bi-Plane! Don't you dare take me back to Old Smoke and leave me to climb round on the steaming metal arse of the Mononstarr. I despise that Willoughby! The man breathes insults!" she threw her arms in the air. "So I'll just unceremoniously die in the jaws of that Limberial Insizor or another Mononstarr Pinion Mouthed Carri-age! That can happen, you know – it has happened! I could easily be shot at by some other stupid, shot-happy Gatherer as well," she placed a hand on his jacketed arm then threw it away. "It wouldn't be bloody fair! I've come this far!"

The exchange gave him reason to pause. Hamish had said it. He was a Gatherer. And although Pen was a technician, she was only a standard citizen. Her lot in Sombre up until now had been so very restricted. No wonder this extremely intelligent girl wanted something else. He stepped away from the her momentarily and canvassed the skies as if they might hold the answer. Hamish said that if he was in Dave's shoe's he would know exactly what he would do with Pen Raines. Drop her back. But he wasn't in his shoes. Dave had control. Pen was willing. It was his decision.

"Ah ..." he scratched his head. "I know I am going to regret this, Pen Raines. But I could use the help – even as short lived as it might turn out to be. Let's have a go at it then."

"I would rather end my time on The Kestrel, Dave," she said in a small but hardened voice.

She certainly had resolve.

86

"Okay, Pen. Thank you. I won't say you won't regret it, because you probably will."

"I need extra protection. We can work on that. *I* can work on that," she said and smiled at him. "So where is your garage, Mr. Dave."

D

"Well, you certainly have a place here, don't you." Pen said looking around his home-base with her hands in her jacket pockets. "Does every Gatherer get this type of housing?"

"No. I wouldn't think so," Dave answered feeling slightly uncomfortable with the question. This had been a secret place for so long.

As if on cue, there was a sudden strum of strings at the doorway of the garage.

Pen turned round and blurted, "Who are you?"

"David, who do we have here?" Sebastien stood at the doorway looking every bit the ostentatious man mountain, dressed in a red velvet robe. He wasn't smiling nor frowning - he appeared to be withholding breath as he awaited a reply.

"Oh, hello Sebastien. Pen Raines, please meet Sebastien Steppanaire. He is my illustrious landlord," Dave said.

"And good friend, Dave. Let's not forget that. Landlord is far too formal for our situation here," he approached Pen with an outstretched hand.

"Sebastien. I am here to help Dave. I am a skilled technician," Pen announced proudly.

The big man's eyes lit up almost hungrily, "Oh, indeed! I should have been able to tell from the coat and the clever look about you! How wonderful for David."

Dave could see Sebastien was performing his version of belittlement. He didn't like this side of the man. Sombre had bestowed wild entitlement on Sebastien - it didn't colour him well.

"Thank you, Pen," Dave said stepping to her side. He peered straight in Sebastien's eyes and took the spotlight away from Pen, "My good fellow. I'm sure I have seen a sort of graveyard around here of old planes, bits and pieces ... you know, from that marauder raid all that time ago. I was hoping we could have a sift through?"

Sebastien gave a short strum then muffled the strings with his right hand. "What are you after, you two?"

"We need to give Dave's plane some advancements. It's a bit on the ploddy side," Pen said earnestly blinking her eyes.

"Well, I wouldn't call it ploddy, Pen," Dave said a little affronted. "It gives amazing service for a Gatherer."

"And if that was all you needed it for that would be fine, Dave. But those Spitfire planes had machinations you haven't a hope to run from ... well, fly from." She placed her hands in her coat pockets and raised her brow at Sebastien, "Can we see this area please?"

He smiled at Dave, and his eyes lit up, "She *is* a very straightforward one, isn't she, Dave?" He considered them both, "Very well my friends. Dave, I'm sure you can find your way. In the warehouse. Ask the staff if you need anything brought back here. They will all help." The big man left the doorway with a strum.

Pen rubbed her hands together. "Very good. Shall we?"

D

The two stood under and within the enormous ceiling and breadth of the palace warehouse. A host of old fighter aircraft had been broken down and left in piles. There was a faint smell of oil and petroleum.

"So all the wings are useless, obviously," Pen said as she walked over and hopped up on the jumble. She climbed a fuselage. "Dave, bring some tools, will you? I'll need your help if we're to get this done."

"Oh, of course," Dave said realizing he had been spectating. He joined Pen on the mound of aero-bits.

"So there are some wonderful guns here, Dave. Of course they are heavy; that needs to be thought about in relation to your bird. To give us a hope of shooting down the enemy we will need at least another two each at our disposal – both mountable. Does The Kestrel take much to control?"

"It basically flies itself once it's settled," he admitted.

"Then you will have plenty of time to aim then ..." She stopped and peered over at the top of another mound. "Oooh! That will be well and truly handy. That's a grenade launcher. We had a variation of the same on The Mononstarr Pinion Mouthed Carri-age'."

"Why would you have needed one on that beastly machine? Didn't it just chew Nightmarers?" Dave said curious.

"No. It performed other dark deeds as well, Dave. Willoughby was indeed an evil fellow if the mood took him. He raged against his own."

"Oh."

"So, all of this is grand stuff. I notice trolleys over there as well ..." She fell quiet for a moment.

"What? What is it?" he said as he began searching through the toolbox.

"Well, your rotary motor is very flimsy, Dave. The Spitfires of The Red Winged Death Command are as you say, around four times the speed. We need to increase by at least three times as much to have a hope – particularly to carry these guns, and some new armour for myself of course."

"What new armour would that be?" Dave was amazed at how quickly ideas were coming to the girl.

"I do figure something that will deflect at least some of the bullets will be in order, something highly strengthened and layered," she said matter-of-factly. "My main problem is the motor on your plane."

"Also the drag. Bi-wings create all sorts of drag compared to single wings," Dave rued.

"Let's not be negative though, Dave, and focus on the things we can possibly change. It's a light motor, a thin motor with just the nine cylinders. I vote we create extra motors, smaller and lighter in design, that work alongside the main."

"Where would you put them?"

"We attach them between the wings. One either side, mounted toward the back struts to assist with balance. You will be surprised how much extra speed can be achieved. The Mononstarr ran on seven motors that powered various areas of its configuration. Of course speed wasn't overly important for that beast, but the mechanics are fundamentally the same. I think two extra radial motors will be the best thing for this craft."

"Why radial?"

90

"Because we actually have them at our disposal, Dave," she smiled. "I am a technician, Dave. Not a wizard. I actually need to have parts to work with."

"Oh, that makes sense." He said realizing how much of a fiddling layman he actually was when paired against a real technical mind. He was grateful for Pen Raines.

She turned to him chewing her bottom lip; her eyes assessed the area some more,

"Can you call the staff? We'll need help lifting these motors."

CHAPTER 15
AT FETID SEAT

The extraction of the motors proved to be not an easy thing. Taking many grunting and complaining servants to assist with the task. Thankfully the warehouse had enough tools, trolleys and chains to get the job done. Pen remained upbeat through it all. Dave did his best to avoid eye contact with any of the servants. He knew it was all quite the imposition. After a long while, there were four wide trolleys filled with dismantled motors and propellers, long and short guns, metal paneling and tools. Everyone present was covered in oil and sweat. No smiles. Dave figured this was much harder than the Steppanaire' servants had worked in quite a while.

Pen canvassed the trolleys then announced, "I am thinking this will be enough now. Thank you. Let's move all of this to Dave's garage."

The heavy trolleys were set in motion two-to-three servants on each. Bringing up the rear, Dave and Pen pushed their own.

A grunting mini convoy crossed the black glass.

"I can't imagine what you're going to do with all of this, Pen. It seems like a hell of a lot?" Dave said genuinely curious.

"Either can I," said Sebastien Steppanaire appearing suddenly at their side. "Hello you two. Just thought I would sneak a peek at your haul."

Dave looked curiously at the large man who in turn gave a strum on his ukulele.

"Well, yes it does seem like a lot. But it in my experience it is best to start with too much then streamline the process as you go," Pen said with a slow nod. "Those motors are a touch large at the moment. I will strip them down so The Kestrel can cope with the extra weight."

"Good. I *was* wondering about tha-," Dave broke off mid-sentence. He received the call from Sombre by way of a shot in the temples. "Well, all of this will have to wait for me I'm afraid – I have a mission. Nightmarer at Fetid Seat - quite the unsavoury and villainous town, I must say. I will have to take my slow old bird with me, obviously." In an apologetic tone he added, "You're not to come, Pen."

"Quite okay, Dave. I realise that. I have a massive amount of preparation to do anyway," she gave him a knowing smile. "Best run ahead and make sure they don't block your way out of the garage with all these trolleys."

"Right you are. Thank you, Pen, for everything."

"Don't thank me yet. We haven't made a single change so far, Dave Bi-Plane."

"We will though," he said over his shoulder as he jogged away. "Make way please! I need to get out."

"Just make it back in one piece!" He heard her call out from behind.

There were no guarantees that he would.

D

Leaving the Steppanaire Air Palace in its wake, The Kestrel soared the Sombre skies en route to The Byway with a boastful display of power. Dave marveled at how well his machine sounded.

He spoke aloud to his transport, "Are you trying to convince me that you're quite fast enough old girl? Ahh ... if that were only the case."

The almighty canal of distorted atmosphere that was The Byway appeared ahead. Dave breathed a sigh of relief. This time there had been nothing on his radio, no sign of the Spitfires. Veering left he steered The Kestrel into the great opening, joining a Balloonist Gatherer momentarily - The Uncanny Cain - searching out his own entry in The Byway wall. Cain' a new addition to the conglomerate (and a little on the odd side if word around The Ruptured Spleen was right). His black hair was oily with a twist, as was his moustache. He cast Dave a quick glance and that was all as The Kestrel powered by.

The Byway roared and wailed in its usual cacophony, he zoned out as his thoughts turned to Pen, working back at his garage. There was still a mightily guilt-ridden part of him that might never be absolved. The woman said that potentially going out at his side and onboard his plane was something she wanted. Pen Raines, no more, serving Dave Bi-Plane's cause. It didn't sit well with him, but she was determined.

With a distinct flicker of sapphire green light his entry presented, and he steered his Sopwith Camel into Fetid Seat.

D

Landing his transport on the flattest surface he could find; on top of a hill, one wheel on a discarded old door, the other sinking in mud, Dave grabbed his lasso, holstered his Exaggerated Pistol and hopped down from the cockpit. Boots sinking in slop, he surveyed the single zig zagging, downward diagonal path of the one and only thoroughfare into Fetid Seat, and further on to the murky waters of the bay edging away at the towns foot.

He had to admit that all of this trouble with The Red Winged Death Command, and the subsequent taking on of Pen Raines, had all but left his real duties as a Gatherer in the shadows. It had been a while since he had any Nightmarer, alive or deceased, to present to The Menders.

"To work," he uttered, and took off down the slippery hillside. Keeping up a careful semi-jog on the slimy road pavers, he entered the street. An unsettling wetness in the air and a smell he would rather not put a name to assaulting the senses.

The housing lining the narrow street were in a collapsed and derelict state. Fit to slide straight into the bay, Dave mused to himself. Many rooves had caved in, walls cracked, some hollowed out, not a window with a single pane of glass intact. A sickly pale light source emanated from most of the houses – signs of clock driven life. His grip on his pistol tightened. The deeper he moved into Fetid Seat the more the sounds of the town presented their ugly voices - faraway crying twisting to screams, unhinged laughter from muffled mouths, throats retching.

A door swung open with a bang. A grubby child stumbled out in a run, roped tied arms bound behind his back, mouth gagged with the same rope in a taught, bonded fashion. A large cut to the head showed bleeding brain matter.

Dave's eyes lit up. What luck!

"You there! Come with me!"

The boy hit a side wall and bounced off. Turning around he faced Dave, laughing through his ropes, as he stumbled backward. A cracked Beating Clock at his chest showed that he was a citizen. "Bleeden dierarghiaaaahhhlll!!!" was the nonsense the young ghoul cried.

"Damn," Dave shook his head as the child ran off down the street bumping into walls.

There was a sudden clatter-roll of metal wheels from behind. "What in all of Sombre-?" He mouthed moving into a doorway clutching his gun. He gaped at the eyeless head of the thing aboard the trolley, a thinly haired creature with just the cut torso melded to the wooden base - Beating Clock stroking at 5. Both arms swung glinting axes with intent, it began yelling through its misshapen mouth. "Oh they come here for their thereafter! It's all under-swept and discarded here! Remnants! Remnants! Oh but the cuts are so painful! PAINFUL!"

The thing made his eyes water. Thankfully it kept on. He knew of Gatherer's that surely would have shot at it. The child from before as well. The jumpier kind among the conglomerate. But what would have been the point? Giving The Menders extra work was meaningless and thoughtless. And Pen Raines's plight was a direct result of such Gatherer stupidity.

The coast was clear. He set off again and the street continued on in its downward concertina fashion. The plan would have to be to search the street and the town square for the Nightmarer first. Entering the collapsing houses would be last.

"And this now?" Dave uttered through his teeth and pulled his pistol once again.

Husky, out of breath voices were coming up the road. "This way. This way. This way. This way. Hurry. Hurry. Hurry. Hurry. This way. This way. This way. This way."

Dave watched them come round the corner and make their way toward him; each on their own side of the street – two burly, hunched oaf-like men running on bare, bleeding feet, pushing empty metal barrows.

"This way. This way. This way. This way. Hurry. Hurry. Hurry. Hurry. This way. This way. This way. This way."

He needn't have bothered with a gun. A quick study of their blackened eyes told him both men were quite blind. They appeared to be on an endless trek around the town, disappearing around the corner, they jogged on, huffing their almost rhythmic chant as they went. No doubt he would see them again.

He looked up and froze. "No. It can't be ..."

At first, he thought he was seeing things.

In the sky, to the north. Unmistakable motors.

Six familiar Spitfires advanced on Fetid Seat.

D

He watched his nemesis descend and land just past the town's beach. How did they know where to find him?

It wasn't unheard of to get to any of Sombre's towns and situations without the aid of The Byway – it just took a lot longer. Too long, he would have thought. Something didn't add up.

"The radio!" he rued the dinky transmitter.

It had to be the radio. Not the first time it had occurred to him. But it just wasn't possible? Or was it? One thing was certain, thankfully, they thought he had the Crystal of Thyst on his person. The Kestrel was in full view, sitting on the hilltop like an adornment. His craft would have been easy to get at.

He heard the motors die. They were about to come at him by foot.

"Dave Bi-Plane! Surrender the gift!" The Strom-Pel pilots of The Red Winged Death Command' yelled in unison, strikingly cold voices echoing out over the town. They were already in the streets. Machinegun fire sprayed, interspersed with heavy stomping bootsteps. "Your demise is inevitable! We will rip the gift from your dead body!"

Machine guns.

"Jesus on a stick!" Dave said under his breath. This mission was very likely to end with his bullet-riddled corpse decorating the ground and another stroke on his clock. He ran onward, feet sliding on the wet bricks. The gunfire was incessant. Were they to shoot every dwelling in the town?

"Bi-Plane! This is never going to end if you do not relinquish the gift!"

The turn of the street ended at the town square. Two shoebox shaped buildings; a dilapidated boathouse and an old brown bricked tavern stood side by side, forming a barrier from the ensuing bay. Water from said bay, lapped up at the road's end.

The abnormal goings on of Fetid Seat stunned in its strangeness.

Googly-eyed, motorized children with laughing, clapping mouths hunted each other with whips in a game of chasey; exposed gears and cog-work in the children's throats rolled their orb-like eyeballs in unison with the mouth. They dodged and jumped around the frighteningly wasted looking, long necked elderly of the town. The moaning skinny men and women crawled along, heads down, licking wet salt from the bricks with wide open, toothless mouths.

A gallows was set at the edge of a deep well. Here was his Nightmarer; a pudgy, purple-faced fellow, hanging from the noose, kicking and screaming choked cries. His business shirt had been ripped open and an X painted on his pale chest. Two women in long dress with featureless, chrome faces stood guard at the gallows, black hair down past their knees. Curiously, both women's hands were chain-bound and holding long heavy swords – Beating Clocks both stroking at 9. When they perished, they perished in pairs it seemed. As strange as they appeared, Dave didn't think they would be too much trouble to dispose of.

His Nightmarer was intact. Choking, but still kicking. He might yet get a clean gather back to Hamish and The Menders.

"Damn it."

The sight of Fetid Seat's bizarre had caused him to forget he was being pursued. A brutal reminder of why he probably wouldn't get that 'clean' gather come upon the square, the 'chikka-chikka-chikka' of machine gun fire coming with them. Bullets punched the atmosphere. Citizens began to fall.

"The gift Bi-Plane! The gift! Your termination will be absolute!"

"Bastards!" He didn't even turn to see what he was dealing with in the Strom-Pel pilots. He ran straight for the boathouse.

The wide, wood-paling door had no handle, just a sawn dark hole – he yanked it open and slid inside.

D

"Oh god, that's awful!" Dave coughed and tried holding his breath as the stench burned his nostrils. A mix of salt and dead and something altogether unnamable. A thing scampered in the darkness.

His blood curdled. He gripped his pistol with two hands. He stood with a boot up ready to stomp on whatever it might be.

Gulping back the need to wretch, he peered through the door hole.

Like so many of Sombre's citizens, the wild and motley collection of ghouls of Fetid Seat didn't know how to fight or dodge bullets from anything outside – they existed to scare, repulse and dismantle Nightmarer's. The square had been shot to pieces. As had his Nightmarer.

The Strom-Pel pilots of The Red Winged Death Command had performed a massacre.

Standing tall with guns in pale, long fingered hands; each wore grey, heavy looking aviator jackets with red striped regalia. The pilots were of human form yet definitely had traits of animal. Bald walnut shaped heads crowning white reptile-like faces, completely devoid of expression. Inordinately large mouths, Dave thought.

"Come out Bi-Plane! This isn't something you can run from!" Curiously, when one spoke, they all spoke, each pilot moving their mouth in unison with other.

There was a fan of useless gunfire that peppered the boatshed's outer walls, thankfully only lodging in to a reinforced inner wall. The taverns windows were shattered

"Ugh ..." Dave stifled a cough, an awfully acidic tickle, that would have surely given up his questionable hideout.

Time passed.

He shivered as sweat formed on his brow. Shifting his feet he watched on as the pilots walked the square – suddenly on heavy shaky legs. Dave breathed a sigh of relief. This was a welcome development. It was if they were struggling to walk on land.

"Boots too big, lads?" he whispered and cleared his throat. They seemed none too keen to venture into his boatshed or enter the tavern.

Low growling came from the pilots; yet there was nothing menacing about it. More like a moaning. He saw one pilot stumble, dropping down to his knees and bare white fangs. Another stopped and proceeded to have a fit. Two pilots hoisted their fallen comrade up and began to walk off.

"This isn't finished, Bi-Plane!" The voices were tired.

It *was* finished.

At least for right now.

The Red Winged Death Command retreated to the main street in a unified stagger away from view.

Dave wrenched the door open and fell out of the uncomfortable dwelling. He breathed the new air greedily.

"Well, that was interesting," he said looking to his brutalized Nightmarer. The man was one big red bloody mess. Bullets had ripped a lot of his flesh straight from the bone. Groaning he got up slow. Stepping over one of the sprawled, chrome faced women, he grabbed her sword and approached the gallows. He climbed the edge of the well-wall and grabbed the noose at the neck.

"Let's get you down, eh? I haven't done well lately. You're my latest failure." He cut the rope with the sword.

The mission indeed was a failure.

He had learned one thing of interest though. His enemy had tired quickly on foot. The Red Winged Death Command preferred to stay in the air.

D

Jasper woke.

His first thought was of Emma Cartwright and Pen Raines.

They were safe.

CHAPTER 16
GRAVITATIONAL PULL

School was just a necessary irritation. Distracted to the point of indifference, Jasper leant on his chin and doodled on the same pad through every class. Teachers would have thought he was paying attention - he was good at showing his 'interested' eyes. There was nothing remotely scholarly behind them though. In the short term it didn't matter. He figured his days were numbered at Massa High.

Seeing Emma after school had been at the forefront of his mind all day. Was he actually interested in her? He didn't think so. Not in the usual way at least. If there was anything resembling attraction that could result in a boyfriend/girlfriend situation, it would be very short lived.

He had overheard his folks at breakfast talking real estate - his mother scanning her laptop and throwing around statements of 'This ones happy for a fast settlement, Tim' and 'Do we want a pool?' 'Three car garage?' She was relishing the task.

Jasper knew his father's enthusiasm was on the increase as well. Making his mother happy seemed to be making his father happy. The settlement hearing was tomorrow 9 am. The move from Arlington to wherever the hell this new place was, was imminent. There was even talk of renting until everything was in order. The Reeves Family Express was rollin' outta town fast.

The final bell rang, and Jasper took flight to the skatepark.

◊

The skies had clouded, the wind had picked up a little. Arlington would get rain. Sipping the last of a Stok iced coffee, the brutally fast sounds of Wehrmacht's - 'Napalm Shower', blaring in his ears, Jasper rolled through the gates of the skatepark. He dropped his bag and the empty bottle. He surveyed the park and couldn't see Emma yet. Dropping into the bowl, he ran some figure eights, scraped the coping hard and hit some warm up airs. Finishing his first run he jumped out and caught his board. Letting a wary looking younger skater go he walked to the seating and sat.

He watched the gate intensely. The afterschool crowd arriving in droves. Scooter kids and skater kids, BMX kids; mums walking dogs with little kids riding in tow.

It was all about to turn into a circus.

The bowl was still empty. He rolled over and dropped in. 'Gone Too Long' by the legendary, Dirty Rotten Imbeciles, drummed his senses, keeping pace with his movements as he thrashed the bowl. A little angrily, it had to be said. Was he frustrated that she hadn't arrived? He knew he shouldn't have been. It wasn't like they had even exchanged numbers or anything.

She might have other things to do.

A voice went off in his head. *'Jasper, calm down. Don't be a needy asshole.'*

Finishing with a 360 air out of the bowl, he rolled along the flat, staring at the concrete. He was suddenly aware of a presence ghosting him from behind.

Emma rolled up alongside and tapped his arm. "Nice air, Jasper. How long you been here?"

They both stopped. He eyed the pale yellow in her cheeks and gave her a smile. Pocketed his ear buds. "Not long. Thought you weren't coming."

"Oh, I just stopped off at the supermarket for some mints. Breath's been a bit harsh today. Smoking between classes - not drinking enough. Thought I would spare you if we ran into each other," she said rolling her eyes and grinning. He liked her smile.

He noticed that she was wearing a little eyeliner. They walked to the seats. Emma sat close. He was okay with it.

"I approve of your Dave Bi-Plane, Jasper. Quite the gentleman, isn't he? This would be the safest Pen has ever felt in Sombre I reckon."

Jasper nodded, "He has that effect on people. Although, I think things are going to get real' deadly soon ... he had a lucky escape from The Red Winged Death Command last night. He actually saw the pilots."

"Really!" Emma turned on the seat and crossed her legs, "Oooh do tell, Jasper Reeves! What are we all dealing with here? They ugly?"

"Heads like white reptiles actually; fangs, slits for eyes. Other than that they look like pilots." He shook his head slowly, "Shot the shit out of Dave's Nightmarer and the town he was at though."

Emma's face lit up, "Hmm. What sort of guns?"

"Machine guns I'm pretty sure."

"Well, while you - woops! - sorry, *Dave* was away, Pen Raines was building a small arsenal. She's damn crafty *and* proactive. Especially when she's happy - I'm finding out ..." Emma looked down at the ground.

There was an uncomfortable silence between them that hung in the air, both understood the meaning. Emma played with the laces on her trainer, the tops of her knuckles nudging Jasper on his upper leg. Again, he was okay with it.

"How long have you got, Jasper? In Arlington, I mean," she said in a low tone.

"Probably not too long. Dad's hearing is tomorrow. I suppose they'll find out how much coin they're suddenly worth and we'll all take off like billionaires in the family jet."

"What, really?"

"Joke," he said giving her a glum smile.

"Ha ..." she mumbled. "Do you know where you're heading to yet? Is it close by?"

"No. It's in California. Some place called Pento."

"Never heard of it," she stopped playing with her laces and leant back on her hands. "Sounds like a shit town." She sighed loudly. "Sorry, I'm just a bit upset is all."

"I know. I'm not too crazy about the idea either. But there's some specialist there with mad skills that can help my father. Apparently, this woman could help him get out of the chair." He shrugged, "At the end of the day, that's all that matters, I suppose."

She shook her head. "We've finally connected though. I mean other than the occasional nod. I've finally got to know Jasper from the skatepark. I like you."

Jasper felt something ping in his stomach. This is what happened when you let someone in. He'd spent most of his days at Arlington dodging this exact thing. Now that he was leaving it seemed it was about to happen anyway.

"I like you too, Emma." He turned and looked straight in her eyes, tried to smile. He was fairly sure it was an awkward one.

She watched him as she still sat back on her hands, "Hmm, well, Jasper Reeves of the skatepark. The mere fact that we needed something as rare as Sombre to happen to know this about each other pretty well means it was never going to ... and now your fucking going away."

"Sorry."

"Don't be. Can't be helped, can it. Sucks is all," she said and straightened back up. She leant in and placed her right hand over his. He stared down at it. That ping in his stomach again, now accompanied by a racing heartbeat. With her left hand she rubbed the back of his neck, then pulled him into her. Her tone gentle she whispered, "Just wanted to know what this would feel like. I've often wondered."

Her lips felt soft. Breath minty. For a second or two, he could have sworn his heart stopped racing and stopped altogether. He gasped when they parted.

She grinned, satisfied, "As good as I thought it would be."

"But I'm going away, Emma," Jasper said. "We can't start this." It felt too good. It was a complication. He watched her mouth. The shape of her lips. Troubling.

"That's okay, don't let that worry you. Just keep me around for a while longer please ... when you sleep, until you leave." She cupped his cheekbones in her hands and brought him in. They kissed again.

Troubling.

D

He now had Emma Cartwright's number. Texts had already been exchanged. Strained ones. From his end anyway. Did he have it right? Were they on the same page? (He really hoped they were) They weren't a couple – just two people with something very strange in common – the nightmare world of Sombre. Whatever it was, it was doomed to only last a week at most, judging by how discussions were heading at dinner.

"There is a rental going at a reasonable rate just out of Lower Pento. Three bedrooms, garage. Low on the ground. We'll take the ramps, while you still need them." Julie Reeves said peering over at Tim Reeves from the laptop. She forked another mouthful of ravioli from her bowl. "You not eating, Tim?"

"Not hungry. Tomorrow's playing havoc on my gut," he said and took a sip of water.

Jasper thought his mother far too cheerful in comparison. He cast a critical eye her way that she was too busy to notice.

He turned to his father, who had given up on his meal completely and was now sitting back in his chair, hands folded on his chest. "So, dad, this person in this place we're going to – she any good?"

He nodded slowly, his tone measured annoyance, "Yes, Jasper. We're not making this decision lightly. You seem to think we are. Am I right? Like its some kind of whim."

"No. I don't think that. But let's be honest, dad. *I* haven't really been considered though, have I?" He did his best to stay as measured as his father. "Haven't even been asked."

"Actually, Jasper. You're right there, not so much this time," he stared daggers straight at his son. Most unlike Tim Reeves. "How's

your legs? They walking you 'round okay? You know, I think they
are!"

"Hey, I-" Jasper tried to cut in.

His father put up a hand. "No. I don't -" he looked over at Julie
Reeves who was watching the exchange with tight lips, "Actually,
correction. *We* don't need your consent. You are a minor living
under our roof and you'll fucking well do as your told!"

Tim looked down at his legs, then pushed away from the table.

"Think you'd better go to your room now, Jas,'" his mother said
shaking her head as she watched her husband roll himself into the
lounge. Eyes tearing a little, she cleared her throat, "he'll apologize
tomorrow. You know he will."

He gave his mother a nod and said nothing.

He left.

ᗡ

After the cataclysmic end to dinner, Jasper was in desperate
need of an aural assault. He threw on Toxik's 'World Circus' album;
speedy 80's thrash metal with an otherworldly guitarist. The intricacy
of the playing like a mind invasion, he opened his laptop and
Googled the town of Pento, California. It looked okay. Big enough –
population 210,000. It had an upper and lower. A decent shopping
strip. A few schools. Green parks. Tidy streets. He couldn't see any
skateparks listed. He knew that didn't necessarily mean the town had
none - they just weren't considered a priority.

Ultimately, Pento had some woman that could hopefully fix his
father. He shut his eyes. He loathed the argument he had with his
dad. All through Jasper's upbringing; they were a team. Father and
son had shared a lot. Not only music; opinions and mannerisms as

well. So similar were they at times, it had made his mother jealous on more than one occasion.

Dinner was just one spat. His father was understandably nervous about tomorrow. Still, Jasper hated it.

He shut his computer down and headed for the shower. Toweling his hair, he saw there was a text from Emma on his phone.

Night, Jasper.

He kept it as short, shorter.

Night.

Throwing his towel on the chair, he fell into bed.

It wasn't just that he wasn't in the mood for pleasantries. It wasn't worth encouraging her. Arlington, and everything in it was coming to an end.

Including anything with Emma Cartwright.

Just wasn't worth it.

He gripped his quilt in his hands and shut his eyes tight.

CHAPTER 17
GROUNDWORK

Jasper could only doze for the first hour.

Recalling the day he'd just had and stressing over the coming days ahead was unavoidable. Images of his father frowning in his wheelchair; of Emma Cartwright's mouth, of stupid Google maps of Pento, California. He fidgeted for a while longer then got up for a pee.

On his return, he thought about boring grazing cows - his go to when he absolutely needed it. His mother had taught him this trick when he was younger. There was nothing more peaceful and duller than boring grazing cows. He watched the herd chewing the grassy field for what could have only been two minutes before he was out.

Sleep.

D

Jasper's screaming was siren like. His body bits were collected roadkill - head and shoulders at the left headlight - the rest, just a mess of destroyed limbs and ribs stuck to the grill. Again, the dream state had him cruelly alive as the car powered through streets he had never seen, along long and empty highways. Night turned to day, day to night. Wind rushed his face and filled his wailing mouth with chilled air. Where was he being taken?

He thought he knew.

To the next place.

The car drove on and on.

D

Dave returned to his garage at the Steppanaire Air Palace to see Pen Raines dressed in quite the odd metallic attire. It looked wildly uncomfortable.

"Pen, what in all of bloody Sombre are you wearing?"

She lifted the cylindrical headwear that appeared to be a piece of tin piping. On closer inspection, the whole outfit seemed to be made of tin piping.

"Oh, hello Dave." She turned and smiled. "All of this stuff clips off. Just testing it out. It's all I had left to use once I'd finished with everything else."

"Looks fairly cumbersome. Will it give you much protection?" he wondered aloud as he watched her unfasten it all.

"Some," she said.

Seeing the engineer without her long jacket on, dressed in just a black vest over a black skivvy neck, he was reminded of how skinny the girl was. Her Beating Clock almost the same width as her ribcage. Her bare white arms thin and insect-like. "You've been working hard, Pen. Can I have the servants fix you something to eat?"

"Thank you, Dave. Maybe later. I want to show you our new guns!" she said with glee.

She led him over to a table where six, stripped down machine guns sat upright on triangular mounts. Inner mechanisms exposed and on display, he had never seen anything quite like them. He thought them quite stylish in their own way.

"Self-loading like everything in Sombre. A lot of what is on a regular gun is casing. I have cut a lot of the metal away and gone with the bare minimum for our usage. I have tested the triggers. They will shoot over a thousand rounds per minute." She rubbed her chin and nodded with satisfaction. She then grabbed his arm and led him

112

toward the petroleum barrels. "And just over here, we have a miniature missile launcher. This is a bit of reengineering and invention that I am quite happy with, Dave. I will obviously man this one. It will be at your back as you fly us."

Covered in oil and grease, Dave marveled at Pen's invention. A rag hung off its two-foot-long barrel. A cord ran from the main body ending with a step pedal.

"You can pick it up," she said. "It's a little greasy is all. I work with lots of lubrication as I build."

Dave reached down and picked up the weapon. It was light yet solid. He snapped down the breach cover and peered through the optical sight. It was such good work. "This is amazing, Pen."

"The barrel is made from hollow axel rod. The rest is from bits and pieces of other old guns that we brought over. It's steam powered. The ammunition is wildly explosive," she said raising her eyebrows.

Dave stifled the urge to laugh. He could see the engineer was enjoying herself greatly. He really hoped all of this business with The Red Winged Death Command wouldn't bring her demise. It already felt like having an eager kid sister at his side. She was a doer. He liked that.

"Of course, it won't be as user friendly as the machine guns. Harder to aim. But when I have an open view of the Spitfires, it should blow them out of the sky rather easily." She turned and pointed to two tarpaulin covered mounds, "Now the motors. I will need your help mounting those."

Dave was in awe of this clever and malnourished girl. He held up a hand.

"Now listen, Pen Raines. Stop will you. Take a break. This is all marvelous. I really am astounded, but you need to slow down for a moment. Let me arrange for some sandwiches and coffee brought to us. You look awfully pale."

She looked down at the floor. "I could eat. That would be nice of you, Dave."

"Go and sit," he directed in a stern voice.

"Okay, boss."

He watched as she pulled her coat back on and walked slowly to the couches.

"Amazing," he uttered.

D

After a brief discussion about Dave's gather in Fetid Seat - in which Dave found Pen was interested in, but not overly. As he spoke, she kept looking over her shoulder at The Kestrel (her singlemindedness to the task at hand he found quite the curiosity). When conversation shifted to the upcoming venture - getting his craft into the air - he had her full attention.

"So we haven't tried anything out yet. How do we know The Kestrel will be able to take the weight of the extra motors," Dave said as he swallowed a sizable bite of his sandwich and sipped his coffee.

"Oh it will cope, Dave. It will cope wonderfully. I would not have produced them if I didn't think so," she chewed her food and thought for a moment, "I estimate we should be able to achieve an extra 120 mph out of your bird. That will help won't it?"

"It will. If it can carry us and all the guns and actually reach that speed."

"The extremely *light* guns," she reminded him.

114

"Well, you will have given me my best shot at least," Dave said and placed his coffee on the table.

"You seem quite negative of our chances, Dave," she looked him in the eyes. "I think you underestimate how much difference having fire power will make," she frowned and got up with a huff, "I've had enough of this sandwich. Please follow me now to the motors. And bring your smile along will you! My god you drivers make me so irritable at times!"

She was right. He knew he had to snap out of it. Being doldrumatic of their plight and speculating on how long she might last would do neither of them any good.

"Right you are, Pen. Coming."

D

The fitting of the motors was heavy work, despite the chain and trolley system Pen had designed to cope with the weight. Both motors had been stripped and streamlined, all seven pistons exposed and shining; propellers had been shortened to suit the width of the Sopwith Camels wing clearance. Original struts were removed and replaced with hi tensile, aerolite bolt-on's, as the motors were X mounted between the top and bottom wing.

Dave was stunned at how quick and efficient the lithe technician worked. Indeed, after the brawn work was over, he couldn't help but feel a little in the way. He assisted with the throttle cables but left the adjusting of the rigging to Pen.

"Amazing, isn't it?" he said. His concerns about the weight of the motors at the wings lessened once they were in. The balance seemed perfect.

"See, Dave. Have a little faith," Pen smiled as she jumped down rubbing her hands together. "Can you please start your machine. I would like to listen."

Almost too eager, Dave stumbled as he mounted the wing and hopped into the cockpit. "Woops! Okay, are you ready, Pen?"

He fired up The Kestrel. A worrying second passed when only the regular rotary started; a momentary magneto lapse as the other two radial engines then roared to life. Adrenalin coursed through his body as he gave his craft more stick. He grinned stupidly at the rush of extra power. Pen's hair fanned out on all angles as the three propellers churned the atmosphere. While waiting for her signal to cut the engines, he spied the large minstrel-esque form of Sebastien Steppanaire peeking round the bricked doorway. He saw that the man wore a scowl.

A grinning Pen held up her hand and Dave flicked the motors off. "They're good, Dave," she said and walked off toward the table of guns. "Let's mount our guns."

Sebastien stepped into the garage. His expression brightened somewhat as he strolled toward them. "Hello both of you. This looks like some busy work!"

Dave gave the man a curt nod. There was something about his presence he didn't like. He couldn't put a finger on why he felt it though. It wasn't the first time; he'd felt this way before. "Sebastien, how are you. Yes, this is our best shot to shake The Red Winged Death Command off our tail. Keep them away from your palace. Pen has done magnificent work."

He raised his eyebrows and gave his ukulele a strum, "Yes, hasn't she. Will it get airborne? Are you concerned?"

"Yet to be seen. It feels right though," Dave answered.

116

With another strum Sebastien wandered over toward the guns and ran a hand over one of the smooth barrels. "Tell me, Dave, how long has been our pairing now? I've lost track of the eons."

"As have I, Sebastien," Dave said jumping down from his plane. He gave Pen a concerned look which she didn't seem to read into at all. The girl just stood with her hand resting on the gun mount, keen to get on with the installation.

"Have you something to say, Sebastien? You know I respond best to straight talking. Please don't circle 'round the point. Is our gentlemanly agreement of my station here coming to an end?"

At first, Sebastien put a hand to his chest and gave Dave a look as if his very words had shot him. Then closing his gaping mouth he spoke, "Well, Dave ... things have seemed to change for you, haven't they? You have this girl here."

"Pen. She has a name."

"Hm ... That surprises me actually," he said.

"Excuse me?" Pen piped up. "I told *you* my name."

Dave raised his voice, "Now, you are being offensive, man! What has brought this on, Sebastien?"

The scowl returned. "I do not like where any of this is heading, Dave! Not at all. I have not made it a secret, n-now have I?" the large man stammered. His eyes were alight, his expression part fear, part anger - "I know they're coming! And I know you're bringing them! Strom-Pel to my very doorstep! AND YOU STILL HAVENT TOLD ME WHAT THEY WANT WITH YOU!"

Dave had never seen him this way. There was an unlikable desperation to his demeanour. Was it unhinged? He retaliated, "Because that is none of your business, Sebastien! I have told you that it will be handled," he gestured to The Kestrel and the table of guns, "And as you can see, we are obviously doing just that!"

Sebastien breathed loudly through his nose as he sneered at them both, beast-like. His delivery was low. "I want this finished, Dave. I want it over with. I want it done."

"It will be," Dave answered looking the man straight in his oddly cold eyes.

The altercation was over. Sebastien Steppanaire turned and left.

"Can we load the guns now, Dave," Pen said sounding scolded. He too felt scolded.

"Give me a moment, Pen, will you."

"Okay," she put her hands in her pockets and watched him.

The atmosphere in the garage had changed. Suddenly he felt unwelcome. The spat had been a divisive one – he knew it. His time at the palace seemed to be coming to an end.

Sebastien Steppanaire had changed. He knew the man had his demons; a mental ledge Sebastien teetered on. Something had pushed him over it. He doubted that it was just he and his battle with The Red Winged Death Command as well. The bloody evil blighters hadn't even approached the palace.

Things were awry.

Taking a look around his garage he breathed, long and deep. "Okay Pen. Let's load the guns. Best we start moving this along."

The two got to work.

CHAPTER 18
CHANGE BECOMES HIM LIKE HANDS REACHING

Jasper woke with a twisted quilt cover in his hands; his heart beating like a double kick drum.

With a cough, he turned over and lay on his back. Blinking at the ceiling he registered what day it was. Trial day. The day the Reeve's got paid.

Change. Change was coming. As much as it was coming for Dave Bi-Plane; it was definitely coming for Jasper Reeves. He peered around his bedroom - at his last twelve years. His family had moved to Arlington when he was three, from some small town in Chicago that didn't matter, and that he couldn't remember the name of. This was the only home he knew. Did the coming change mean *everything* was about to change? Arlington was his foundation. It was where he found Sombre and Dave Bi-Plane. Would he lose the connection to the airman when he moved to Pento? Dave still had eight strokes left on his Beating Clock and Jasper Reeves wanted to be there for every last one of them.

He coughed again. With a groan he got out of bed.

Trial day.

D

The kitchen was alive with nervous energy as Jasper sauntered in and pulled some bread from the cupboard. He dropped two slices into the toaster and slid the squeezy honey along the bench.

"How'd you sleep, Jas,'" his father said from his spot at the table. He was dressed in a suit. He looked sharp. "Can we leave last night behind us, bud? I was being a bit of a dick. Sorry."

"Sure," Jasper said not looking up from the toaster.

"We'll keep you posted through the day." His mother said in a tone rich in falsetto. She was excited. "Probably have take-out for dinner. You can choose."

"Money'll be no object, I suppose," Jasper said snidely.

Neither parent bit back. The toaster popped; he spread some butter and squeezed enough honey to drown both slices.

"Sunday morning we thought we'd take a drive out to Pento and check the town out, Jas'. Need you to come as well, kiddo," Tim Reeves said. "We've rented a small place until we decide on a house to buy in town. We'll stay overnight. You'll miss school on Monday."

He looked up at them both. His mother hid behind her coffee mug. She was annoying him greatly. He wasn't about to fight the request though.

"How long's the drive?" Jasper said as he chewed slowly.

"Around six hours. Make sure you pack a night bag," his mother answered.

"Okay."

"Good. Your dad has his first meet and greet with the new therapist before we head back here."

"Her name's Sue. Never met a Sue I've liked before. But she's meant to be the second coming, so we'll see ..." Tim Reeves joked.

His mother rolled her eyes, "Thinking your mispronouncing there, Tim. Fairly sure its spelt X-i-u. Seeing as though the woman is Chinese."

Jasper watched his mother and father as he swallowed the last of his toast. His mother went to scrolling on her phone with her left hand; her right was placed on his father's wrist. There was definitely a union between them that hadn't been there for a while. It had to be a good thing. His mood lifted a little. Maybe it wouldn't be all that bad.

"Anyway. Send me a text when you're done. Hope we get what we need," Jasper said as he got up from the table.

"Thanks, Jas. It'll be okay," his father said with a wink. "What you been listening to lately? Who's at the top of the pile?"

"Spermbirds probably," Jasper said as he backed out of the kitchen.

"Something To Prove/Nothing Is Easy - their best two ... don't know what happened after those albums," Tim said shaking his head.

"True. The other stuff sounds a bit thin," Jasper said in agreeance. "Anyway. I'll see you guys later on."

He left.

D

Lunchtime, Jasper sat in the school cafeteria chewing his way through a Health&Co Lean Bacon Salad Wrap, washing it down with a bottle of strawberry Yoo-Hoo. He thought he'd needed the extra sugar, although it was making him feel a little ill. It wasn't often he sat in for lunch at Massa, but today he did. Kind of a Friday-last-lunch-ever sort of deal. Was it his last day at the school? Maybe. He felt like it was. He took another sip, continued to watch his fellow students as he listened to the full album of Gorilla Biscuits 'Start Today'; short, sharp, energy clocking in at 24 minutes total. Awesome. One of his father's all-time favorites. Civ, the vocalist, shouted and spat the lyrics with passion and urgency – as if his life depended on it. Something most kids his age didn't get at all. He watched them all blurt sentences, whisper and laugh at whatever, eat like pigs and go out of their way to fit in; make friends with people they may-or-may not agree with or even like. They could consider Jasper a loner and probably did - but they could never accuse him of being follower.

Deciding there really wasn't much at Massa he was going to miss, he got up and left the cafeteria. It was a decent sort of day. A little breezy, a bit of cloud and enough sun to make someone want to be out in it. He scrolled through a few messages on his phone. A text from his mother; the trial was over. A settlement reached. A smiley face at the end. His mother was happy, which meant the Reeves's were happy. The primary influence of the mother. He responded with a 'Yay'. Shaking his head, he looked at two other messages from Emma, 'U there x' and 'PTB x'. He wasn't great with messaging; actually forgot it could be done most the time, such was the tendency to go straight to his music. 'Sorry been busy see u at park.' He pocketed his phone, shut his eyes and tilted his head skyward for a few seconds as he walked.

Emma Cartwright and Pen Raines.

The technician was on her last stroke in Sombre. She seemed to want to sacrifice it to Dave Bi-Plane. Dave was a standup guy. He wouldn't let Pen perish surely.

Everything in Jasper's existence, be it awake or dreaming, seemed to be scrambling to a final axis point. A definitive end. He felt a pang of nervy energy in his gut and burped up whatever sauce was on that wrap.

The bell rang. Two more classes and he was free of Massa for another week. He breathed the air and headed to class.

D

Arlington Skatepark. If there was one thing he was going to miss, it would be this. The bowl was one of the smoothest he had ever skated - and he had skated plenty.

Before his accident, Tim Reeves had still skated himself - on the weekends. There had been many a car trip; father and son, stereo blaring old school skate-punk, thrash and hardcore. About as enjoyable as anything ever got - Jasper's favorite part of his upbringing.

He would love to miraculously lift this bowl out of the ground and somehow take it with him. He dropped in on it again and felt the smooth concaves, his wheels grip the concrete as if they were one. He aired and landed and relished the grip he felt. As good as the bowl was - if the move to Pento meant that he might see his father back on his feet, even back on his board one day – losing the bowl was a small price to pay.

From the corner of his eye he saw that Emma had returned from practicing her street across the way. She now sat on her board watching him, rolling one of her cigarettes.

Jasper stopped at the base of the bowl with one foot on his board, killed his music and peered up, "You know, they'll age you, don't you? They're not a good thing."

She lit up and puffed a waft of smoke. "It's okay, Jasper. Once you leave me, I'm gonna quit. Shame you won't be around to see it."

"Well, good I guess," he said and hopped up out of the bowl. He sat on his own board alongside her. She put her hand on his knee and blew her smoke away from him.

"So, hopefully I will see you tomorrow. Then you'll be off to this new town for a visit. Correct?" She squeezed his knee prompting an answer.

"Yeah. Back on Monday," he said staring at the tear in her jeans, the frayed white ends. "Don't know what's happening after that. It's all happening pretty fast."

She butted her cigarette out in a ridge in the concrete. "That it is," she sighed and wiped the corner of one eye with her index finger. She cleared her throat, "I blame you. You know that, right?"

"What do you mean?" He continued to look down at the tear. Fixating on the torn fabric, he began pulling on a strand.

"Well, to be honest, if you hadn't been so fucking closed off for so long, Jasper Reeves, I could have gotten to know you sooner." She pulled him into her chest and kissed the back of his head. "You're pretty cool, you know. I like you a lot."

Her grip was strong, as if she didn't want to let him go.

"I know. I like you as well. I just never thought I needed anyone else in my life, you know?" Jasper lifted his head and they kissed.

When their lips parted, Emma was the first to speak, "Do yourself a favour Jasper. Don't do that. Its selfish. Let someone in occasionally. It wasn't just Sombre that caused this you know. Maybe it gave us a push, but it's not like I wasn't known to you. It's not like I didn't try."

His natural guard against complications. It was a stupid thing he realized. This was a missed opportunity. "Should we try and keep in touch?"

124

Emma loosened her grip and let her arms slide away. She cleared her throat, "Ah. No, Jasper. We really don't. It will be too hard."

She was blinking fast. He could see that her lashes were wet. She rubbed her eyes with the back of her hand. She cleared her throat, "Let's meet up again tomorrow. Maybe let me know where you're at next week. I will want to see you when I can until you go. You and Dave need to keep Pen alive awhile longer is all."

Jasper looked down at the empty bowl.

Symbolic of how he felt – hollow. "Okay."

Emma stood up and adjusted the neckline of her top, "It's been bizarre if nothing else, anyway. I'll never forget it. I'll never forget you, Jasper Reeves."

She bent down and kissed his forehead. Jasper caught her hand; the skin felt smooth and a little cold as she clasped his fingers. "I'll sort of see you tonight, eh? Hope Dave Bi-Plane's on his game. My Pen's a good girl. See you, Jasper."

"Tomorrow," Jasper said and let her go.

He watched her skate away.

CHAPTER 19
INTERMINABLE FORCE

Champagne. Jasper had been given a nip as well. A small third of a flute.

"To new beginnings!" said a beaming Julie Reeves.

"I'll second that," Tim Reeves said straightening his back in his chair.

Glasses were clinked. Jasper sipped with his mother and father.

"Ugh!" he gasped at the taste.

"Ha! Guess we won't need to worry about you raiding the liquor cabinet for a few years!" his mother chortled.

"No. That's awful," Jasper grimaced poking his tongue out in disgust. The label on the bottle said the champagne was French - he figured the French must enjoy bubbly, fruity urine.

The doorbell rang.

"Oh. That'll be the pizza," his mother said placing her champagne down on the dining room table. She strutted to the door.

Her father watched her with a smile. "She's happy, Jas'," he said to his son.

"Are *you*, dad?" Jasper said with a raise of the eyebrows.

"I am if she is, Jas'," he turned and looked up at his son, his face read contentment, "moving's a big pain in ass. But you know, I need to get off 'mine' and out of this chair. For me and for you both. If we need to travel a state or two to do it, so be it."

"Man, these smell good," Julie Reeves said on return.

126

The Reeves's sat down to eat.

D

A few hours later, after web chatting with a bunch of like-minded friends on his favorite forum, ThrashCoreSkateinc., belly still full of too much pizza, Jasper showered and readied for sleep. There had been no texts from Emma. All quiet there. He pictured her leaving him earlier - rolling off toward the skatepark gate. She was plenty sad, he knew it. He felt bad, worse than he thought he would.

It was never going to go anywhere.

"Should never have started anything up ..." he grumbled and flicked the light switch off.

Standing in the darkness he listened. The dark made everything quieter; yet made the thoughts in your head louder. Flopping onto the mattress, he pulled the quilt up to his chin. Loud thoughts continued; an invasion of problems raged, racing toward the forefront in a bid to take over his mind. A displeased Emma Cartwright leading the charge, followed closely by the impending upheaval of the Reeves's move to some place called Pento, of losing the Arlington skatepark, fearing the distinct possibility of his father never getting out of his wheelchair despite the move to a new town to make it happen. He grunted loudly and fanned unwanted heat out of his quilt, kicking his legs up sharply.

"Jesus!"

Forcing himself to think of those boring grazing cows, he shut his eyes and slowed his breathing.

Those boring grazing cows.

Minutes passed.

He fell asleep.

D

Jasper's body jerked spasmodically on his mattress as his Rite of Passage nightmare continued on ...

His wild night ride, stuck to the grill of the black muscle car, came to a screeching halt at the foot of a short bridge. The exhaust grumbled. The driver of the car revved the motor hard, then harder again. The radiator spat copious amounts of wet steam at the grill. Jasper's body boiled; his bones, his flesh and sinew liquefying and turning to a gory soup that dribbled down the bumper and poured out to the tar. Jasper's neck and shoulders were the last to fall, punching the road like an overripe tomato.

Face down on the tar, he tasted the asphalt.

Having cleansed Jasper from its body, the car backed away and he was left.

Somehow able to peer up, through one jellied eyeball he read the sign at the top of the bridge. WELCOME TO PENTO - *Jasper Reeves!*

He had arrived.

This wasn't the end. It was a beginning. Suddenly there was movement within his liquification. Sensation began coursing through his spilt mess. Jasper Reeves was to go on.

The first to reharden and re-calcify were his teeth; he bit into the road awkwardly with his top layer until his chin, then jaw, followed suit and his face was lifted. His neck then hardened through his spine - within seconds he had a backbone; then ribs, arms and legs through to his feet. The reanimation of Jasper Reeves was complete - re-skinned and re-boned, clothed and ready.

128

He stood ... and crossed the bridge into town.

'Where are you?' he called out as darkness filled the landscape ahead.

Ɒ

Dave Bi-Plane had always felt a modicum of control with his lot in the nightmare world. Not a lot to fear. Predictably unpredictable, every new day brought new conquests, new gathers, new Nightmarers. There was always the risk of an axeblade to the head, being shot at close range, getting ripped apart by one of any breed of creature at any juncture. Any interminable variety of unsavoury nastiness could befall him – but this went with the job - any Gatherer worth his or her salt knew this and accepted it gladly. If there was a fear, it was only what was shared by each and every citizen of Sombre. Attrition. The stroke rate on The Beating Clock. And he had that fairly well in check for himself. Only four down. Eight to go.

As he sat at the helm of his beloved biplane, he felt like control had all but been lost. Never had he been responsible for anybody's precious twelfth and final stroke. Pen Raines was sacrificing her existence to help him fight; a fight that was his own fight alone.

And sadly, he wasn't especially good at compartmentalizing, (His great drinking friend, fellow Gatherer, Halliday Knight, was wonderful at it) for him it always had been a bit of a chink in his mental armor - if the engineer perished, he would feel it.

He searched for and found some resolve. This was just a blip, an intermission in his existence.

But it had to end now.

Turning in his seat he called to his co-pilot, "Pen Raines, are you ready?"

Surrounded by her skeletally built, yet undoubtedly effective mounted machine guns, Pen lifted her visor on her cylindrical tin helmet and spoke through what she called the Talking and Listening Pipe.

She cleared her throat, "Ready, Dave."

The badly named device worked well. He had his own. Fastened to the inner of the helmet, the arc shaped copper device sat just away from the mouth and rested smoothly on the earlobe. The mechanisms that allowed such a device to transmit a signal between them both was an absolute mystery to Dave. Just like everything the Old Smoke technician had managed to do for him so far.

"Then let's head off!" he said with excitement and fired up The Kestrel.

Three motors roared to life. Dave gave his craft some stick, and they moved from the centre of the garage. He gave his housing a final glance. "I have a distinct feeling that this will be the last time I will be in this garage, Pen."

"That is a shame, Dave. It is a useful workshop. But I wouldn't think you would miss that string-playing-Sebastien too much. He was rather rude and petty the last he spoke to us!" Pen answered loudly over the motors' echoing caterwaul.

"Yes," Dave replied as they drove across the black glassy surface of the grounds. To the north-east, at the palace entry, along with a few servants, Sebastien Steppanaire stood watching them both. No ukulele in hand this time; Dave could just make out the scowl on the man's dial, the glare in his eyes. Their relationship was now tainted. Dave was on the outs. He had brought a threat to the man's shiny palace. It didn't seem to matter that he was setting out now to set it right.

130

Realizing he was stalling, Dave focused on the task at hand. Turning the biplane back around he readied for takeoff.

He pushed the stick all the way forward and The Kestrel built speed rapidly. The shaking from the extra horsepower almost too much – overkill. His stomach lurched in a good way as any concern of drag from the extra loading was quashed. Reaching the edge of the glass his craft launched like it never had before, throwing him back in his seat, soaring higher and higher into Sombre's skies.

"You-are-a-bloody marvel, Pen Raines!" he yelled as adrenalin pumped in his veins.

"Thank you, Dave! The working relationship in these motors are not so far apart, you know. Now you have the extra power and fuel efficiencies of two radial motors supporting your machine's original rotary. The gearing of both kinds are quite complimentary to each other."

"Well, it is impressive, Pen. Much like the builder," he said sure that the compliment would give her cause to smile under her silly tin helmet.

Dave lowered The Kestrel to an approximate three hundred feet above The Common Ground. The blue-grey skies were relatively empty of Gatherer balloon or airship. Just one balloon, with a turquoise coloured envelope heading out from The Byway, pilot and what looked like the slumped body of a Nightmarer aboard.

Unbeknownst to him, it was the last scene of normality.

"How is this going to go, Dave? What should we expect?"

Dave turned to see the technician in practice; grabbing each of the four guns, swinging and aiming them on their gun-mounts. He smiled a little uneasily. She seemed a bit of a deft hand; definitely no stranger to a weapon.

"I have no idea," he said as he turned back around.

Sombre had its ways of forcing the inevitable, this he knew.

The skies ahead were empty and calm.

Eerily so.

Dave knew it to be not a good sign.

There was a sudden dryness to the air; licking his lips he swallowed. He shivered. In the pit of his gut he felt it; it had crept up on him. He saw The Kestrel's gauges had all bottomed to zero.

"Oh bugger it all."

Everything had changed ... and he hadn't noticed.

They were flying in a void.

"Actually, Pen, get ready. We're heading to Strom-Pel."

CHAPTER 20
STROM-PEL

There was no actual known way to Strom-Pel.

For an aviator down on his or her luck, it could only come about. Finding themselves suddenly in its path; a one-way ticket to bedlam.

Although, this had nothing to do with good or bad luck. Dave knew that Strom-Pel had come upon he and Pen Raines because it was time. The Red Winged Death Command wanted him in their air.

Dave watched the skies ahead, he spoke into his Talking and Listening Pipe, "I'm not going to sugarcoat this Pen. This is now a suicide mission. If either of us come out of this intact it will be a miracle."

"I don't wholly agree with you there, Dave Bi-Plane. It's time for us to fight, that is all," Pen said and fired a single practice shot from one of her guns into the atmosphere. She added sharply, "Please stay positive for me. I've worked bleedin' hard for this!"

He didn't answer her back.

As if a great and mighty hand threw a blanket over all of Sombre, the sky turned from blue to a hellish black-red. Hot driving rain began to fall. A fiery vortex opened ahead as a tail wind rushed his craft from behind.

"Hang on Pen!" Dave shouted as he was thrown forward in his seat, face planting the control panel. He watched the speedometer dial arm suddenly climb from zero to the uppermost top.

"Pen! Hold - I'll try and-" he said starting to black out as he braced himself on each wall of the cockpit and fought the wind rush. He got upright in his seat only to have his craft sent into an involuntary barrel roll as the maw of the vortex sucked The Kestrel in.

D

"Dave! Are you alive? Dave?"

He stirred at the sound of Pen's voice. He then felt a prod in his back. It hurt a little. She hadn't fallen out. That was a relief. He opened his eyes - had they been shut? That was new. He had blacked out? That was new as well. He had never done that before.

"You need to fly us Dave. We've recovered," Pen Raines persisted, "c'mon now. We'll crash into something."

"Yes, sorry Pen." Still giddy, he took the control in one hand and steadied. He veered the biplane left and avoided a floating, horribly mangled fuselage of a passenger jet.

"Pen, how is the equipment, do we have everything? These bastards will be all over us soon!"

"I lost some tools when we were spinning. My fault, I should have fastened them to something," the technician rued. "I'll just have to hope everything stays intact." She added, "This is all quite the depressing floating graveyard, isn't it?"

"It is - Ugh! Blast it all!" he added tetchily.

He realized just how uncomfortable he felt. His clothes were drenched from the rains, water ran down his chest, probably rusting his Beating Clock, his body temperature kept shifting from feverish chill to coursing heat. He rolled his shoulders and grimaced, "It's all bloody awful."

134

The legends of Strom Pel were accurate. As far as the eye could see - aviation hell and ruin, en masse. The stench of a myriad of fuels and gases burned the nostrils. Wrecks of every description hung suspended, ghoulishly haunting the air; deflated dirigibles with empty baskets, burnt out airship skeletons with gutted engine rooms, twisted 'copters turned slowly in morbid pirouettes. Unattached motors with idle propellers; demolished cabins and air-lounges, gargantuan jet turbines yawned and wailed on severed wings. Everything a testimony to the horrific side of aviation; all broken and ripped open, all torn apart and adrift.

Dave flew The Kestrel onward through it all.

Diving down and under a monstrous DELTA airliner's still burning fuselage, he turned round to see Pen, visor up, mouth agape, staring in awe at the great silver air-whale's undersection.

'Of lies and deceit, of secrets and a parody of existence! Dave Bi-Plane, you are a liar and a thief! Strom Pel holds a place for airmen who cheat the inevitable!'

He whipped his head back around. The words were so scathing! More than a little affronted he yelled, "Well, that is a first! I have never been called a liar or a thief! Ever!" He was being exposed and wrongly accused of an untruth. Where was this all coming from? He turned to his co-pilot and coughed out a too high pitched, "Pen, do not believe a word of this!"

She didn't react.

'Hand over the gift, Bi-Plane! It belongs to another! You disgusting liar of an airman.'

He shifted in his seat and canvassed Strom Pel for any sight of the red winged Spitfires. This was to be a game of cat and mouse.

'You filthy liar, Bi-Plane! How you deceive them all!'

Pen remained quiet in the back.

An enormous twelve valve engine appeared in The Kestrel's path and he deftly rolled them clear and straightened.

"Pen, are you alright?"

"I'm fine, Dave Bi-Plane," came the taught reply. "Just fine ... steer the plane."

"Okay. Stay focused then," he said knowing full well she wasn't fine.

'Liar. Thief. A coward that cheats his own inevitable demise!'

"Okay - enough!" Pen piped up. "Actually, Dave Bi-Plane, no I am not!" she cleared her throat for extra resonance.

He sunk in his seat.

"Have I been helping a liar? A felon? Have you stolen something! Jesus, man! There *has* been a bloody secret you haven't told me hasn't there! I've felt something about you, you know! But you have posed as such the gentleman that in my stupid gullible way I have ignored it! What is this gift you have stolen?"

"I haven't stolen anything!"

"Well, you obviously have!"

"No I haven't, Pen. The gift was *gifted* to me. I have never stolen so much as a beer nut!" He added in a lower tone. "They are after my Crystal of Thyst."

"What?"

"Don't make me repeat it. No one is meant to know of its existence." There was silent pause from behind as Dave steered them round a hideous, splattered and stretched human form plastered against the nose of an airliner.

"It's what keeps me safe in The Kestrel. I will never lose a stroke on my Beating Clock while I have it with me."

"So how is it that The Red Winged Death Command know of it?" she said accusingly. "That is quite the hole to fill in your story, Dave Bi-Plane!"

"Do you not think I haven't asked myself that very question a hundred times since all of this trouble started? If there is one thing I can do well, it is keeping a secret ... obviously."

"Yes, obviously," she agreed her tone simmering. "Okay then, Dave, then there is something or someone else involved here. Do you think the mighty Sombre itself might have relayed its existence to these miscreants?"

He looked above briefly before he answered. Darkness was setting in.

"Why would it now? It happened upon a Dave Bi-Plane long before my version of the man. I just recall how the exchange went and guard the damnable thing! Hold on!"

Skillfully rolling his craft' left around a yellow bi-winged, De-Havilland Tiger Moth, (a biplane many considered superior to his own Sopwith Camel – he didn't agree). As if showing off, his three engines responded with a satisfying bellow as he then dropped into a full barrel roll, narrowly avoiding a grim looking Cessna. Levelling The Kestrel, he flew hard and fast and pierced the needle between a burning silver bomber and a neighboring airship, each setting the other aflame in some bizarre fire battle of extinction.

'Closer! Dave Bi-Plane! Closer!'

A squadron of eight murderous looking F-105 Thunderchief's soared diagonally in unison over Dave's little flyer, jet engines creating an unimaginable din. As they vanished from the skies of Strom-Pel, a wobbly and stunned sounding Pen Raines spoke her thoughts. "Well, let's thank our luckiest that those beastly machines are not after us. We would be quite the spec of pigeon shat in the wake of those. Grand monsters indeed!"

"Yes, flashy," Dave said intentionally underselling the jetfighters. "If you really want true grandness, take a look below. I would guess this is the real Strom-Pel."

A gargantuan oblong structure hung in the atmosphere. At its centre, a temple shaped control tower floated amidst a flaming sky cauldron as it oversaw eight levels of tracked runways. All manner of aircraft landed and readied for takeoff.

Dave fretted, "We're not meant to come back from here, Pen. You know that don't you. This is a pilots damnation. Oh, I'm sure Hamish and The Menders will get The Office to me somehow as I have strokes left on my clock' ... but you-"

'Dave Bi-Plane. Surrender the gift now and your demise can be avoided.'

An announcement sounded from the control tower, a woman's voice, the tone warm and surprisingly professional, the message callous and pointed. 'Red Winged Death Command are clear and ready for takeoff – take no prisoners. Bring Dave Bi-Plane to the fires of Strom-Pel. All hail Strom-Pel. Hail!'

Spitfire engines roared; machine guns fired as The Red Winged Death Command ascended from one of the lower levels of runway.

"Dave! We need to turn back!" Pen yelled into her Talking and Listening Pipe. "Are you in a stupor? Please, we need to go, now!" She opened fire with two machine guns.

He was as his co-pilot said he was – in a complete stupor - hopelessly mesmerized by Strom-Pel and mesmerized by the sight of the six Spitfires hurtling his way.

His eyes glazed. His hand limp on the control stick. He knew he had to act. The enemy was close and getting closer. Yet it all seemed to be happening in slow motion. It definitely wasn't the time for soul-searching, yet he was unable to stop himself. He wasn't a fighter pilot. He was a Gatherer. How had this all come about? *Why* had this all come about? Why? The unfairness of it all. Causing him to enlist the services of this poor girl, valiantly firing away in the back seat of his shitty little mode of transport. He was using her. Using her to fight an enemy he had never had before. Sure no other Dave Bi-Plane had either.

'There will be no escape from Strom-Pel, Bi-Plane!'

"Who is responsible for this, Pen?" he said out loud. He turned and watched as her small, tin armored body shook with the recoil from the machine guns.

"What?!" she said incredulous. "Jesus, Dave! Get us out of here!"

The Red Winged Death Command were closing in. Two hundred feet away, one-fifty.

Nothing remotely in slow motion now – it was all happening brutally fast. As fast as the black spinning propellers of the menacing Spitfires.

"Ooooo! I got one!" Pen yelled.

A staccato run of bullets then peppered the length of The Kestrel's fuselage. "Dave, they got us on the side!"

He was stunned into action, "Hang on. That's not meant to happen. Does the crystal not work here?"

Pulling his own gun round, he pressed the blip switch down hard and all three engines responded. He sent them higher, climbing the air, The Kestrel raged, leading a race with its hungry devil's close behind.

"That's high enough, Pen. Hold on, I'm inverting us. Push your legs against the walls to brace yourself." Dave said as he levelled the plane upside down. Pen adapted straight away.

"That's better, Dave! Stay like this! I'm going to take one out. Get ready for the boom!" she said as Dave skillfully flew them upside down, balancing the stick and blip, firing his own machine gun, his bullets pinging off a propeller of a front runner.

From the corner of his left eye he watched as Pen rested her rocket launcher across her breast and shoulder.

'We can maim you terribly, Dave Bi-Plane, the gift is no good to you here!'

The Kestrel pushed hard right as Pen fearlessly launched the rocket. It was a direct hit. Devastating for the enemy as a Spitfire instantly caught fire at the nose and spiraled out of control. It crashed into another Spitfire tearing a wing straight from the body. The two planes plummeted down, engines wailing, exploding in mid-air.

"Luck, Dave!" she yelled excitedly.

"My god, Pen Raines, what is in those rockets!"

"A measured mix of Chlorine Trifluoride, Dave. We used it as a cold coal starter in Old Smoke. Coal was always wet in that awful place," she stated not able to stifle a giggle.

"You didn't tell me about that," Dave marveled as he watched the fiery planes plummet to wherever a crashed plane ended up in Strom-Pel.

The four remaining Death Command pilots rolled away in pairs to the left and right. He and Pen had struck a blow.

Dave felt The Kestrel stutter.

"Let's get us the right way up. Are you okay, Pen." He straightened and the motors settled into a better rhythm.

They were heading into an ominous red sky; clouds obscured most of what lay ahead.

"I'm okay, Dave. A little thickheaded from blood rushing to my cranium ... dead plane ahead," she added most matter-of-factly. Dave skirted them round a large grey and corroded cargo plane. Doors blown open, every bit the holey air carcass.

"They can hit us, Pen."

"I know. They said they can maim us terribly. There are holes lodged in your craft just below my seat. So I agree."

He bit into his lip. He was angry – not at her.

"No. Please hear me now. They said that the gift, my crystal, is no good here. I am thinking The Red Winged Death Command have no real interest in the thing! Why would they need it? There is someone else involved. I bloody know it!"

"The mystery will unravel, Dave. But stay focused, man," she said in her offhanded way. Her brazen indifference to their peril astounded him, he also found it comforting.

"You'll have to fly us well. We need to stay out in the open if we can. That way we'll be able to take our best shots. We have the armament and I'm all warmed up now."

Thunder clapped the sky as a sudden rain began to pour.

"This weather might cool your trigger finger somewhat," Dave said as he zig-zagged them round a slew of wreckages. "The bloody weather in this damnable place!"

The screaming wail of the Jericho Trumpet signified a second wave of attack. What was left of The Red Winged Death Command were coming in fast from above.

CHAPTER 21
A TRUTH WINDOW TO RUIN

Crashing thunder brought a state of unbridled urgency as everything turned wild.

'Bi-Plane! This isn't over!'

The Red Winged Death Command came screaming downward at The Kestrel. Rolls Royce engines like roaring sky lions, machine guns sparking in a drumroll of spitting hate.

Dave and Pen returned fire.

"This damned weather!" Dave yelled as he looped-de-looped his plane dangerously at 300 miles per hour. The enemy followed suit, matching the aerial maneuver with assured prowess.

"Stop worrying about the weather, Dave. It's more than futile, man!" Pen shouted back as she moved between gun mounts. There was a distinct pinging of tin. "Ouch! They got me."

"Where?" Dave fretted.

"The tip of my stupid tin helmet. My visor is jammed now ... oh, they'll pay for that! Mark my words!" She yelled.

Another slew of bullets peppered The Kestrel, "Keep moving us around, Dave, or they'll shoot your tail clean off!"

Dave shivered at the helm as a chill coursed through his chest. He admired Pen's pluck, and they had been lucky so far, but luck would run out, he knew it. Four against one. The odds severely stacked against them. Another Spitfire motor blew out as a Pen Raines direct hit blasted another. "Yahhhhhh!!!!!!" she kept firing. The enemy plane rolled upside down, the canopy dropped opened and the Death Command' pilot fell out into the Strom—Pel atmosphere.

Dave felt a bullet puncture his right shoulder, tearing through the leather and lodging in. Pain surged through to his fingers. "Ahhh! No! No! My shooting arm! ... I've been hit, Pen! I think it hit a nerve. I'm on one arm for the rest of the battle."

"Just fly us, Dave. Speed up. I'm about to launch another rocket!" the brave engineer said thrilled, "We're winning!"

It didn't feel like they were winning, not at all, but he hit the blip and The Kestrel responded, diving down, smashing through the basket of a limp air balloon. The haphazard move causing the balloons envelope to drape the front of another Spitfire, catch the propeller and send it into a momentary spin. "Dave, faster! That plane's all over the place. We can't let it hit us!" Dave flew them faster; the cabin shook, all gauges to the maximum and quivering, rain blurring his goggles.

"Now!" Pen said finishing the Spitfire off with a straight and devastating cannon blast. Fire ripped through the fighter from nose to tail. "Four, Dave! Could you have ever imagined! Four!" Pen cheered herself on.

He was in shocking pain and no doubt bleeding profusely under his jacket arm, but Dave smiled a little.

Pen Raines was an amazement.

The last two pilots of The Red Winged Death Command veered off, diving into the darks of Strom-Pel.

D

"How's the old girl holding up?" Dave said looking down the sides of his beloved Sopwith'. He answered his own question, "Not so bad by the looks. Surface wounds. They haven't hit any of the motors yet."

The rain had stopped, the skies of Strom-Pel had quietened – as had Pen Raines. Dave let her go. He thought the girl deserved a bit of quiet. She would be exhausted.

When she finally did speak, it was one of the sweetest, unforgettable things he had ever heard from any one citizen of Sombre.

"It's been amazing Dave Bi-Plane, really, it has. Taking me on like you have has meant everything to me, you know." She cleared her throat. "You ... you are such a wonderful man. Old Smoke was filled with the most loathsome, filthiest beggars imaginable ... it makes you wonder what it's all about at times. Our existence here in Sombre hasn't much light shone on it, does it. Twelve strokes and you're out like a poof of smoke." She paused. "Well, I just wanted to let you know that whatever happens - you've shone a light on mine. That's a fact."

"Pen-" he began, but she cut him off.

"Shhh! Hear that, Dave? They're on their way back. I can't see them though."

He would've loved to have thanked her properly, tell her he felt exactly the same way, but the moment had passed. "Yes, I mean, no ... I can't see them either."

The now unmistakable sound of those Spitfire motors were on approach and closing in; though the skies were frustratingly clear. Both Dave and Pen scouted Strom-Pel but there was nothing.

"Dave, this doesn't feel right. Can you see anything yet?" Pen said, ready with hands on her triggers.

"No I can't. It is unnerving," he agreed as his right arm began to quiver from his bullet wound. He gritted his teeth.

The motors faded.

"What are they playing at!" Dave growled as he dropped The Kestrel down under the same burning passenger-plane they had passed on their way in. "Are they now playing fly games with us?"

"Yes they seem to be. They've stopped taunting you as well I've noticed. A diminished fleet has certainly shut their lying mouths," Pen huffed then added positively, "I think we might come out of this victorious, Dave. I think we have them covered."

She was grinning behind her dented helmet, he could tell. He just wanted her safe now. She had done more than enough.

"I may just outlast this and come with you on one of your Gatherer missions."

'We swore that this would be done, and you have gotten in the way, gunner!'

"Pen!"

The deafening roar of the motor horrific from such close range. The deceptive game The Red Winged Death Command had been playing was over.

No more games.

Rising, black propeller spinning wild, the Spitfire's left wing crashed and snagged The Kestrel's tail, upending the smaller plane. A chain was slung, and a hook pierced the tin of his craft and locked it to the Spitfire. A lone grinning pilot appeared over the wing, machine gun in hand. *'No more, gunner!'* Spraying bullets the pilot slid from the Spitfire and mounted Dave's biplane, straddling the fuselage. Bullets pinged away at Pen's hopeless armour.

146

"Ahh!" Dave took another hit to the lower back throwing him forward into the control panel. Though, the bullets were not meant for him. The Kestrel twisted and rose with the enemy plane, then dragged through the air like caught rubbish.

"Dave! Dave!" Pen screamed as the other remaining Death Command' plane came in from the side, guns blazing the body of The Kestrel. The ambush was brutal and executed with perfection.

"No you-!!!" A suffering Dave Bi-Plane managed to get himself upright. He turned. "No!" No, Pen!

He saw the blade in the Death Command pilot's white hand.

He saw the savage and sick grin, baring sharp fangs.

Then he saw the decapitation of Pen Raines.

D

Face wet with tears of anguish, he screamed as he fired at Pen's killer with his machine gun, "You filthy bastard, leave her!"

The pilot leapt or fell from his plane - Dave couldn't tell which. And it didn't matter.

Pen Raines was finished in Sombre. Dave had failed her. He couldn't look at her remains. He just shut his eyes as his motors died; his shattered craft was dragged through the air by what now seemed a most formidable force.

He kept them shut, even as the atmosphere changed and a new light shone over The Kestrel's battered tin panels.

D

The Spitfire's Rolls Royce motor was really a beastly thing - a V12 Merlin - liquid cooled, powerful and as dependable as a handclap. Any aviator worth his salt knew this. Dave had failed in the face of such a motor despite his efforts – using and killing a great technician and comrade in the process. He listened to the Merlin's thrum and roll, then the shift down in gearing as it finally landed, dragging his Sopwith Camel behind with an uncomfortable hop that made his bullets wounds pull and sear.

Dave dropped his hands from his face and looked up.

"What?"

He was utterly mystified.

The black shining glass of Sebastien Steppanaire's Air Palace. "What?" He repeated stupidly.

The Spitfire's canopy opened, and the lithe form of the pilot appeared. A machine gun was pulled out and pointed in his direction. "The gift, Dave Bi-Plane."

He looked down at Pen's corpse for the first time, he tasted bile and let out a cry. "Jesus! What in hell is going on here?"

Sebastien appeared, his movement uncharacteristically quick and officious, stomach bouncing under his robes as he made his way across the glass with ten servants in tail, all with heads down.

Dave felt the bile rise again.

Sebastien shook a fist in his direction, "Now, Dave Bi-Plane! You heard the fellow. Surrender it. Surrender it now!"

"Sebastien? You? You're behind all of this?"

He kept one eye on the barrel of the Strom Pel pilots machine gun. "Why? Of all the betrayal! How do you even know of it? I mean ... I've never-" he rose from his seat.

The pilot stepped closer, he spat in his reptilian tone, "Back down, Bi-Plane."

148

Sebastien eyed the pilot and smiled darkly. He stood at The Kestrel's wing and peered up. "I would suggest you do as this fellow says. They are quite the evil breed, as I am sure you know by now."

Dave sat back in his seat, "Not one to talk now are you, Sebastien. Look at what you have done." He gestured to Pen's corpse. "You pig of a man."

"Oh, let's not start hurling insults at each other, now Dave. I just want what should rightfully be mine," he glowered, "Now give me the Thyst."

"Rightfully yours? What in all of Sombre makes you say that, Sebastien? Seriously, are you really unable to function knowing that someone has something you haven't? You have everything! Do you deserve any of it?" Full of spite he added, "Greedy bastard of a man aren't you."

Sebastien stared directly into his eyes and spoke in a knowing tone, "McAdam Von Freign ..."

Dumbfounded, Dave could only continue on staring back.

"... Of Monolyth, Dave Bi-Plane."

"How did you know?" Dave said.

"I have always known. At first, I was able to accept it. But please know that it is not just pure greed, Bi-Plane. You see, McAdam Von Freign is meant to be a distant relation. Although we have only had rare contact. Monolyth being as hard to find as it is." He shook his head slowly, "McAdam is an incorrigible twit of the far-flung-mystical that should have never had such a gift in the first place!"

Dave shrugged, "I see. That doesn't really tell me why you think you deserve to have it though does it now?"

"Because it needs to be in the hands of a collector, a possessor with stature! And I have waited for this as long as I have known you!" He gave Dave the darkest smile imaginable. "That's right. Our friendship has always been a ruse. A staging of the highest order. "Now hand it over! I will have this fellow here shoot you in your seat, man!"

Dave was astonished at the length the man had gone to; their whole arrangement a lie. How had he not seen it? He had been completely blindsided. Regardless at how he felt, he wasn't about to give this bloated deviant any such satisfaction as witnessing his own shock.

He held steadfast.

"Then you will never get it," Dave said in reply then added, "and I will come back renewed from a mending and destroy your palace." He wasn't at all sure that he would definitely do this, it did sound impressive to say such a thing.

Eyes wild Sebastien screwed his mouth up. "Where is it! Where in the hell is it!"

He instructed the pilot, "shoot his arm off."

Sebastien's servants turned away as the pilot opened fire. Dave was thrown back in his seat, screaming as bullets punctured up and down his left arm. The limb finally gave way at the shoulder and hung limply inside the torn leather sleeve.

For a moment Dave couldn't breathe, the pain excruciating. Blood ran from his sleeve, pooling on the floor of The Kestrel. He hadn't felt pain like this for some time. He was a rare Gatherer - a marvelous preserver of his own wellbeing. Not since the loss of his third and fourth strokes had he felt such excruciation.

150

"No! Stop!" he cried out doubling over. Coughing hard enough to dislodge something in his chest.

Indeed, things had gone his way for some time.

Now Sebastien Steppanaire and The Red Winged Death Command were about to claim his fifth stroke. Rocking in his seat he shut his eyes and spat his words. "A-Alright s-top it. S-top it ... alright."

It hurt far too much to talk, but he had one last thing to say.

"I-I need Hamish t-to bring The Funneling!"

"What? What are you saying? Hamish the Mender? Oh my dear man, he will only be required well after this is all done," Sebastien said. "Get me the bloody Thyst now, Dave, or I will have my cohort here shoot your left leg off as well."

Dave only had hate for Sebastien Steppanaire at this moment – extraordinary hate. Not because he'd had his arm shot off, not because the coward got everybody to do his dirty work, not because he paraded around like some happy idiotic minstrel when he was anything but, and not because everything he had arranged had gotten the wonderful Pen Raines beheaded.

No. It was his greed.

He hated Sebastien for his undeniable greed and what lengths he would stoop to in order to get what he wanted. The man was a crazed, self-serving megalomaniac! Everything Dave hated in a citizen.

"You've gone quiet, Dave? Have you nothing left to say to me? No fight left?"

Dave groaned, "What ... Ugh. And what is left to say to you, Sebastien?" His wounds stabbed at his nerve endings, he fell in and out of consciousness, Dave bent down under the control panel and reached for The Crystal of Thyst. He snapped the metal cover off and felt for the leather pouch. It felt so small in his fingers, insignificant and not at all worth the trouble it had caused.

"True. I have and always will get what I need. The great and remarkable always do."

Dave got himself back upright in his seat only to collapse sideways like a drunkard. He had lost so much blood. He was tiring badly, "And what ... makes - what makes you so great and remarkable? Here-" he slung the pouch with a flick from his wrist. It fell to the black glass. "Have the stupid thing."

"Careful you fool!" Sebastien scrambled madly for the crystal shoving a servant sideways in the process.

Dave saw the shimmering glow of The Funneling to the north of the palace grounds. Hamish had answered his call. A first Mender appeared, a familiar looking woman - summing up the scene she headed back into the magical corridor obviously to make a report to Hamish. It was rare for The Office of The Menders to arrive when things hadn't been resolved.

Sebastien Steppanaire obviously thought things *were* resolved. He stated off-handedly as he shuffled off, "Well, I have it now. Clean yourself up, Dave Bi-Plane. Never grace my palace again. Servants, come."

It all happened far faster than Dave could comprehend.

The servants didn't follow Sebastien straight away.
Instead, all ten drew an Exaggerated Pistol each.
Then they followed.

The gunfire was deafening as bullets opened Sebastien's skull and bloody polka-dot stains appeared all over the large man's back. He crashed heavily to the black glass. The palace staff kept shooting until they passed by his corpse. All ten guns were then dropped, with hollow sounding, metallic clatter.

The staff continued on to their place of residence.

D

Everything then turned very unreal for Dave Bi-Plane. The rattle of a chain, the warm thrum of the Spitfire's beastly Rolls Royce engine, all the sounds fading as he succumbed to the absolution of a Sombre citizens temporary oblivion.

The very last thing he heard clearly was Hamish the Mender's voice,

"Dave Bi-Plane's body first please. We need him back in business."

CHAPTER 22
SHIFTING VOCATIONS

Jasper had spent all of Saturday down at the Arlington skatepark. The day after Dave's failure to keep Pen Raines in Sombre. There was no sign of Emma Cartwright.

He sent plenty of texts her way for a total of zero responses. Was this what happened once your time was over in Sombre?

It all just went away?

Saturday night's sleep had been relatively low-key compared to the cataclysmic one he'd had on Friday. As per usual, he couldn't recall what his Rite of Passage nightmare entailed.

Yet typically, everything Sombre related was as clear as if it happened a minute ago. Dave Bi-Plane had been stuck on the chrome table at The Office of The Menders with Hamish. Much to Dave's chagrin, he had lost another stroke.

When he came-to from his mending, the chief Mender cleared a few things up for Dave.

The servants actually shot Sebastien Steppanaire as a directive from Sombre. The almighty power that was Sombre put the Exaggerated Pistols in their hands and directed the execution. Sebastien's greed, his god-complex, was out of control and taking up a Gatherers valuable time from the vital task of gathering Nightmarer's was unforgivable. Pen Raines was to float in The River. Dave never saw her again.

D

Pento seemed alright to Jasper Reeves. It was a large town. There were shops. There was a wealthy part and a not-so-wealthy part; Upper Pento and Lower Pento. After the lengthy drive, Julie Reeves continued on and drove them round on a bit of a sight-see.

"There's a bakery – that looks nice. Oh, and a couple of salons. Look, there's a- ... actually I can't really tell what that one's about." She seemed to be hellbent on announcing every shop she saw as if everyone in the car was blind. Jasper watched on through his window as Suicidal Tendencies full discography continued stomping away in his ear drums. He occasionally took a bud out of his left ear to comment when he saw something of interest. There was a reserve and a park with a basketball court and thankfully, some sort of skatepark.

"Bowl, Jas," his father said from the front.

"Saw it. Good," he responded.

The school he was to attend was Centurion High. Looked fairly well built and newish, and from the front at least, appeared larger than Massa'.

As organized, his father made initial contact with his new therapist, Xiu Chen; she worked out of her home in Upper Pento and seemed nice enough – 'she has accreditations up the wahzoo,' his father had said well impressed.

As the day was ending, Julie Reeves parked them out front of an estate agent and picked up a key. "Key," she stated waving it at them both grinning as she started the car again.

The small house his mother had rented them was a bit on the old side but would do for the short term (just the one bathroom everybody noticed and commented on). Jasper threw his bag down

on his strange new bed and tried texting Emma again. For the twenty
fifth time.

She hadn't answered him once.

〇

Take out for the Reeves's was Coke and kebabs with fries on the
side. Jasper the only one to finish his meal, such was the overly
generous helping of spiced lamb.

"So, we'll know where to go if we haven't eaten for a couple of
days beforehand," Julie Reeves laughed as she plonked the balance of
her kebab down onto the table. "Should have grabbed a bottle of
wine." She stifled a burp after a sip of her drink.

Tim Reeves smiled at his wife as he wiped his hands on a
napkin. "Julie. I think I'm going to like it here." He turned to his son,
"Jas, what say you? I mean, so far at least."

"No complaints. Pretty good. They have a skatepark. Should
have brought my board."

"Okay then-" Julie stifled another burp, "-sorry, Coke. I think we
don't prolong the move here. Tomorrow we get back home, grab
everything we need temporarily and return. The rest of our stuff goes
into storage, saw a U-Haul up on the highway not far out of Pento."
She smiled raising her eyebrows as she looked around the room.
"Pento, eh?"

Jasper had to admit it was all a bit exciting.

〇

A night in a strange house. A strange bedroom. A strange
bathroom as well. Jasper watched his reflection as he brushed his
teeth. He still had the yellow in his cheeks. The demise of Pen

Raines and the apparent vanishing of Emma Cartwright hadn't caused it to disappear at all. If anything, it was stronger in colour.

He huffed as he spat toothpaste into the basin and rinsed.

Lying down on his sheets he pulled the quilt over, shut his eyes and placed his buds in ears.

Agnostic Front's punk anthem, 'Gotta go', took off in his ears. Quite fitting really, he thought to himself and smiled.

Sleep came to Jasper Reeves. His Rite of Passage nightmare into Sombre attacking his subconscious as always ...

D

It was a fine blue-sky-day. He was walking. The street was crowded. Live music played in the distance. A festival. Barbecue and fried food invaded his nostrils. Sweet, sweat and savory. And people. People everywhere.

He looked skyward. A biplane flew above, motor farting away like biplanes tended to. It carried a long, tied banner along behind creepily reading, **WELCOME TO PENTO! BUT YOU SHOULD HAVE STAYED AT HOME JASPER REEVES!**

He stopped walking. He looked to the people of Pento. Their eyes began bleeding. Every last one of them, blood running free down cheeks and necks. Suddenly he realized they all carried knives. Every last one of them.

The sound of inhuman screaming from hundreds of voices as he was set upon. Stabbing.

Pain gave way to darkness.

D

Dave Bi-Plane eyed the parking at the base of The Unexplained Mountain as he flew The Kestrel down. He saw Halliday Knight's mare, Wilder, meandering around under the tree it seemed to favour a lot. This made him happy. A drink with Halliday just what he needed. Still rather raw after his rebuild; the woman's stark bluntness would fill the small void left from Pen Raines's demise. As he pulled the plane up in mid-air and prepared for Copter mode, he eyed the back seat and sighed. The technician's silly tin pipe helmet had pride of place. On the rebuild The Menders asked if he wanted to throw it away. He said no. It was all that was left of her work. The extra motors were gone, the guns; The Kestrel was restored to its former, adequately capable self.

Dave dropped his craft down between a Speed Truck and a grouping of Tensioned Ratioed Speed Cycles. He hopped out of the Sopwith Camel's cockpit feeling light and energetic, the way one always would for a short time after a rebuild. He was on his fifth stroke now. He had to guard it. Strokes were too precious to give away cheaply.

He walked to the lift at the base of the mountain. As he took the short journey upward, he adjusted the new silver chain around his neck. At its pendant was the Crystal of Thyst – the stone not entirely comfortable as it kept knocking against his Beating Clock. Hamish had pried it from the dead hand of the greedy, Sebastian Steppanaire.

It was Dave's after all.

The elevator door opened, and he breathed the atmosphere. He could definitely go one or two of his lagers. He stepped to the double wooden doors and entered The Ruptured Spleen's usual rowdiness.

D

"You know, sometimes there is nothing better than a decent mending. You do seem rather well for it, my Dave," Halliday Knight said as the two peered over the bar's outdoor bannister at the goings on of the carpark. "Something good came from all that trouble, you look dapper, man!" Halliday laughed then hiccupped. She put a palm to her mouth. "Oh dear, probably had one too many of these wonderful mixes this eve'. I thought that well-meaning bungler, Orty, was a little off when he poured me the first two – Scotch to Dry and all. Five down now, I think I may have called out his shortcomings too early." She turned round, leaning her back against the bannister. "Let me breath for a spell, my Dave. Then I shall saddle up once more for another."

Dave gave her a knowing smile, "Would not be the first time you would have accused the man of a bad mix, Miss Halliday." He took a long swig of his lager and watched her purse her lips and expel air. He thought her such a great beauty, drunk or sober.

"You know, Halliday, I don't think I have ever come across a citizen of this ruddy place like Pen Raines. I shall miss her greatly. Good and pure and rare she definitely was." He took another sip.

Halliday furrowed her brow. "Oh, really my Dave? Purer and rarer than I?"

"Well, other than your good self of course," he nodded and smiled.

She returned the smile then looked at him thoughtfully, "Dave, do you ever think of your own troubled sleeper at all? Do you ever wonder what they are up to, how they might be going with all of this?"

"I do but I don't dwell on such things," he admitted.

She shook her head and gave him an incredulous look, "My word man! Do you even know the fellows name? I am assuming he is a male? You all know of mine. My bloody Hope Kelley haunts me like some rampant graveyard spook!"

He glanced down at the remnants of his glass, "Well, yes, I do Halliday Knight. Ha! Surely after all this time you don't take me as an ignorant." He grabbed her empty glass from the bannister. "Let me go fetch us two more."

"What is his name then, my Dave," she said folding her arms. He was sure the woman didn't think he knew!

"Jasper Reeves ... I am Jasper's Dave Bi-Plane. There you go. I also sense he is on the move."

"Oh? And where would that be? I am impressed you know this about him, my Dave. You are a man of surprises and many mysteries you are."

"Where he is meant to be, Halliday. I can feel it."

The two exchanged a look.

There was an undeniable truth behind it.

A coming truth.

Dave fetched the drinks.

A note from the author.

I hope you enjoyed reading Dave Bi-Plane 'Fights the Red Winged Death Command' as much as I loved writing it.

Just a side note,

Grimprint Publishing with its two titles to date **'Sombre'** and **'Dave Bi-Plane 'Fights the Red Winged Death Command'** are independent releases and an independent venture. I love good feedback and to know you guys are out there. Please show your support by leaving a review on the various online platforms – Amazon, Goodreads or whichever online bookshop you may have purchased from.

In doing this it encourages others to consider picking the books up themselves. It's a massive help!

Thank you

Website - sbnorton.com

Goodreads - goodreads@s.b.norton

Amazon – search the titles and leave a review!

Email – s.b.norton.author@gmail.com